CHUN

CHUN

A Novel

David Ollier Weber

Kila Springs

Kila Springs Press is an imprint of the Kila Springs Group, Placerville, CA.
E-mail: press@kilasprings.net

This is a work of fiction. Names, characters, places and incidents are products of the author's imagination or are used fictitiously and are not to be construed as real. Any resemblance to actual events, locales, organizations or persons, living or dead, is entirely coincidental.

The instructions, symbology and commentary on the I Ching *are excerpted and adapted from* The Book of Change: A New Translation of the Ancient Chinese I Ching (Yi King) With Detailed Instructions for its Practical Use in Divination, *by John Blofeld (George Allen & Unwin Ltd., 1965).*

First Edition, First Printing

ISBN-13: 978-0-9716481-6-6
Library of Congress Control Number: 2012907813

For Christine and Nicky

CONTENT

Unseasonable spatters of May rain rattled across the cabin roof.

They came in gusts, driven by a fierce wind. The wind rushed through the trees around us—fitful, ominous. The rip and crash of a falling branch nearby had awakened me. I rolled over and squinted toward Sharon. She still seemed to be sleeping.

After a while I crawled out from under the blankets and lit a candle. Eddies of damp air siffled through chinks in the walls. The flame hunched low, smoky, hugging the candle's protective rim.

Although tradition demands that it be stored shoulder-high, the book was among those piled beneath my writing table. It wasn't hard to distinguish, wrapped in a woman's embroidered silk handkerchief I'd bought for the purpose from Goodwill. I slid the book from the pile and grabbed a small bamboo brush, a bottle of India ink and a pad of yellow ruled paper from the tabletop. I fetched a stick of incense and a ceramic holder from the windowsill.

I knelt in the center of the room, my back to the table. I was facing north, as directed. I blew on the floor and passed a hand lightly over the boards to brush away dust—leery of spinters. I unwrapped the book. Paradoxically, for all these ornate trappings, it was a used paperback with coffee stains and rumpled end pages. I removed the three coins tied in a corner of the handkerchief and arranged everything properly: candle, book and coins squared to the cushioning silk; incense holder centered in front of the book; brush, unstoppered ink bottle and paper placed neatly to one side, at the ready.

I bowed—kowtowed—three times, according to instructions. What the hell. I lit the stick of incense in the candle flame, inserted it in the holder and picked up the coins. They were tarnished Japanese fifty-yen pieces struck of some dull metal that, from its flat ring when dropped, made me doubt it was precious. The coins had holes in the center. They were souvenirs of my last WESTPAC cruise to Yokosuka four years earlier. Somehow, even though alloyed and a nationality off, yen seemed better suited than American coins to Asian divination. Besides, they were not, at least around here, negotiable.

I had already framed the question clearly while lying in the dark. Now I shut my eyes and concentrated hard, passing the coins through the incense smoke three times as I moved my cupped hands in a clockwise circle. In for a penny—well, fifty yen—in for a pound: Might as well throw the I Ching the way The Man recommended.

I jangled the coins to mix them and let fall.

The first toss was two tails and a head. That signified a "static" yang line, according to the book. I dipped the brush in the ink bottle and drew it on the paper, like this:

I tossed again.

A "50" and two flowery faces. They bore the kanji for Japan, Nihon, about the only kanji I still recognized. So I'd thrown what the book called a "young" yin:

The third toss gave me three heads. That was a "moving" yin line.

When I had thrown six times, my hexagram looked like this:

I consulted the book's table of numbers, found the lower trigram, Chên—which means "thunder," "movement," or "a quickening"—then ran my finger across to the upper trigram, K'an—which means "water" or a "pit." That gave me the number of my hexagram:

Three.

I leafed through the pages to Hexagram 3:

CHUN.

I'd learned, from a "Table of Approximate English Phonetic Equivalents of the Names of the Hexagrams" in the back of the book, that the word is actually pronounced "Jwên." The little tent over the e means the vowel is "so short as to be almost non-existent." So. "Jwnh" or something, kind of a grunt. Whatever. The headline told me this hexagram means, quite simply, "DIFFICULTY."

I frowned and grunted.

Inauspicious.

However, there was a footnote:

The fundamental idea of this hexagram is that of birth and growth amidst difficulty, as with a sprouting seed becoming a young plant and

11

forcing its way through the earth. Our affairs, being still in their early stages, are vulnerable; we must not wander forth, but attend to them until they ripen; then, with proper care, the seed will bring forth a splendid tree. The upper trigram, a pit, suggests a need for caution; but, if we heed these omens, our success is assured.

My frown had somersaulted into an awed smile. Once again I was amazed by the I Ching's *uncanny responsiveness. "...Birth!" No far-out, vague, omnioracular Delphic pronouncements here. And*
    "...Success assured!"
    Let us hope.
    I scanned the text avidly, and then the Confucian commentary:

Difficulty: When the Strong (the celestial forces) and the Weak (the terrestrial forces) first unite (to procreate something new), the birth that follows is not easy. Yet, to those struggling upward from the pit of adversity, determination to follow a righteous course promises great success. As when the universe was first created amidst the fury of thunder and rain with everything still primitive and obscure, this is a time to strive unceasingly for consolidation.

Because I had obtained moving third, fourth and sixth lines, I checked their meanings:

FOR THE THIRD PLACE: Pursuing a deer without a guide, the hunter finds himself lost in the forest. The Superior Man perceives that he must stay where he is, as going forward would lead to trouble. COMMENTARY: His lack of caution in hunting the deer resulted from his being too set on capturing it. The Superior Man always desists when to advance would bring disaster.

FOR THE FOURTH PLACE: Hesitating like a man trotting to and fro, he waits for marriage. Thenceforth, good fortune will prevail and every action prosper. COMMENTARY: To pursue what we desire, that is wisdom.

FOR THE TOP PLACE: He hesitates like a man trotting to and fro or like one shedding blood and tears. COMMENTARY: How could a flow of blood and tears endure for long?

I considered what I had read. Although directly applicable to the context of my question, the injunctions were necessarily subtle. Figuring out their precise meaning always calls for care. Right-mindedness.

The ideal approach, according to the book, treads a tightrope course between rational analysis and blind intuition. If anything, though, one should lean toward the latter. Skirting, however, the urge to indulge wishful thinking.

Ah well.

I calculated a second hexagram, according to customary procedure: Moving lines—young, unstable lines—are considered to be undergoing metamorphosis into their own opposites. So my new hexagram looked like this:

Li—"fire," "brilliance," "beauty"—was on the bottom, Ch'ien—"heaven," "male," "the active principal"—was on top. This combination yields Hexagram 13: "T'UNG JEN: LOVERS, BELOVED, FRIENDS, LIKE-MINDED PERSONS, UNIVERSAL BROTHERHOOD."

I squinted at the text.

> Lovers (friends) in the open— success! It is advantageous to cross the great river (or sea). [Footnote: To make any kind of journey.] The Superior Man will benefit if he does not slacken his righteous persistence.
>
> COMMENTARY ON THE TEXT: This hexagram indicates that someone weak comes to power, occupies the center of the stage and responds to the creative force. Such a one is called the beloved. What is

described in the above text is the work of the creative principle, which has a strong refining influence. The central line (in the upper trigram) to which all the others respond, symbolizes the Superior Man; he alone can carry out the will of all the people of the earth. [Footnote: A strong and gifted person must sooner or later take the helm and guide that weaker person, wife or ruler.]

SYMBOL: This hexagram symbolizes heaven (the sun) and fire representing a pair of lovers. The Superior Man treats everything in a manner proper to his kind. [Footnote: An analogy, based on the component trigrams, between the sun and fire, which to some extent are of a kind.]

So there I had it.

I shook my head. Weird stuff. But truly fantastic. Of all the sixty-four hexagrams I could have come up with, those were the two I got.

I grinned and glanced over at Sharon, slumbering heavily in the shadows.

Something new to mull over when I sidled in beside her.

A fresh tattoo sounded across the roof. I bowed three times and refolded the book in its silk.

HEXAGRAM 1

CH'IEN

THE CREATIVE PRINCIPLE

...Vast indeed is the sublime Creative Principle, the Source of All! It causes the clouds to come forth, the rain to bestow its bounty and all objects to flow into their respective forms. Its dazzling brilliance permeates all things from first to last....

Thursday was clinic day, so we got up when it was light.

You're supposed to be there at eight. Sharon made a pot of green tea and heated some brown rice that was left in the bottom of the pan from the night before. A lot of times we sleep late in the mornings, but it's always nice to watch the day get started. I squatted outside on the bare ground and sipped the hot tea. A thick autumn fog was billowing through the crowns of the eucalyptus trees. You could hear the moisture slithering down the leaves and dripping into the underbrush. It was the kind of damp, early-morning sea-fog that usually burns off by about ten. The clumps of grass around the clearing were crystal white, and the dust under my toes was cold and compacted. A bunch of bluejays were squawking, darting back and forth in a very businesslike way, scratching in the twigs and just generally being obstreperous. They're the bank presidents of the bird world, I mused: always impeccable in their proper blue suits, cocky and self-important, avid to foreclose on other birds' real estate, gobble up their nest eggs and stuff. I tossed a couple of blobs of rice in their direction. The jays didn't seem interested. It was still kind of chilly, so I went back inside and got a sweater. Sharon had already put on her boots, and a cotton print dress that was way too small around the belly now, and a heavy belted cardigan that had been woven by Aztecs or Incas or somebody. I put on my boots. As usual, it took about twenty minutes to get the car started.

The trip to the county hospital is pretty long, especially since our hard-used little *deux chevaux* won't even coast over forty. But it's a nice ride down from the hills. The road is narrow and winding, with a sheer face on one side and a deep gorge on the other. Tucked in the vee of each cleft, far below, are

21

lush pocket valleys. Around every hairpin turn there's a view to sea. When it's foggy overhead, which is almost always in the mornings, the ocean looks frigid. The grey rollers crash white against the snaggly black rocks offshore: colorless, arctic scenery. When you get right up to the coast cliffs you can sometimes spot seals in the water. Sharon let out a yelp and pointed toward a pebbly corner of beach. She said she saw an old bull lounging there. I leaned across her but couldn't make out anything. Her stomach got in the way. Besides, I was supposed to keep my eye on the curves ahead.

We got there at eight-twenty. We were last in line. The gherkin-faced clinic aide who registered Sharon made a big fuss about how we had arrived too late and how we would have to come back next week and how we would have to be there on time when we did and all. The fact that we'd had to drive nearly fifty miles didn't seem to dilute her astringency any. But when Sharon said she was in her ninth month and threatened not to return otherwise, the babe reluctantly let us sign in. We sat on a long wooden bench against a wall for three hours and grew intimately acquainted with each minute crest of our ischia.

There were maybe two dozen women in the room. Each of them seemed to have about five kids, all under the age of four. The place was a planetarium of infants—galaxies of them, like so many graduated asteroids, looping and colliding on their eccentric orbits about stolid central mother suns. The women were mostly Mexican. Or more accurately *chicana*. The coast range is furrowed with warm lettuce valleys and nearly every town has its sewerless back-street *barrio. Colonia.* A constant mutter of Spanish spiced the clinic air. A few husbands were in the room, looking bored and reconciled to boredom as only a chronically jobless Indian-Iberian can look. I guess. There were some Negroes. Not many live in the county. There was one other... hippie couple. We passed the time eyeing each other diffidently.

22

Actually, I use the word "other" with some reservations. Sharon and I don't really consider ourselves hippies. For one thing we're too old—or anyway I am. I'll be twenty-eight in December. Sharon's the right age, I guess—twenty-three. But it seems to me her life-style is shaped pretty much by mine. And I'm a pre-hippie. I have a history. Have you ever met a hippie carrying around a history? I mean, in a way I must admit I'm just living out a life-style—make that *Weltanschauung*—I absorbed from Kerouac and Ginsberg back when I was wearing sneakers and dropping out of Santa Clara. I mean, I'm kind of an updated beatnik, I suppose, obsolescent as that may make me.

For example, I like to read. I've seldom known a hippie who could tolerate print, at least in anything greater than immunogenic doses. And for another example I like to drink. Alcohol in its various forms can produce a very pleasant social high. Sharon and I drink wine. We also drink beer. Consider that agriculture apparently developed from man's aboriginal desire to have a supply of fermentable grain on hand at all times. And yet hippies are always putting down booze. Peyote and mushrooms and ganja they dig, because the holy Indians have burrowed into consciousness with those natural tools since time immemorial. But what about the quintessential sacrament—C_2H_2OH? Ah, cchhoh! Just because their portly papas toss a few martinis down the gullet every night to escape the terrifying psychic consequences of managing the Chevrolet Better Buy Used Car franchise in Turlock or something... I mean that's no reason to dismiss alcohol out of hand. It's a logical fallacy—I forget which one.

But then, so is my generalized assault on the hippie stereotype. That couple across the room—he in his Black Bart Stetson with silver Navajo band, his drooping mustachios, his leather vest and denim shirt, his knee-high fringed rawhide moccasins; she in her ankle-length gingham dress, her horse-blanket shawl, her beaded squaw band around snarled blond

23

hair—who was I to say that they had not just, indeed, digested the entire ten volumes of the *Story of Civilization* by Will and Ariel Durant? I don't like to be categorized. Why should I do it? I mean that's the whole bag, right?—to live, if possible, outside categories. To be merely human. So: Hair grows (this, of course, is pretty superficial) from the male face... let it. Hair grows (coaxillary proposition) from the female armpit... let it. Hair grows: Let it. Be a *homo sapiens*. Be a free person. Groove with life. (Great Philosophical Utterances of Western Man Number Twenty-Eight.) You're in the world for sixty-seven-point-two actuarial years, or whatever. Enjoy it.

Oh Dick, see Spot run. See the trees. See the sky. See the sea. Oh, look. Look, Jane.

Yes. Aieee, I do dig it!

And so one is categorized. Sharon and I are hippies. We live in a cabin in the hills. She makes pots and I write poetry. I've even published, twice. We come to maternity clinic because we have fucked and borne fruit and have no money. We sit for three hours on hard benches and occasionally stroll outside to smoke hand-rolled cigarettes. We watch the homunculus in her belly quiver. And finally she is interviewed by the public health nurse and gets to see the doctor.

Afterwards we drove down to the fishing pier and bought a few handfuls of squid.

There were only a couple of boats in. The squid are an unsolicited bonus in the fishermen's nets. They practically give them away. Sharon's not so hot for the suckery tentacles and oozing ink and little parrot beaks and baleful eyes. She watched a pelican cruise while I uncrinkled three ones and handed them to the skipper.

The sun had come through. The air was tangy with salt. The water was blue out to the horizon, but an opaque fog bank still lurked there, waiting to hitchhike back on the evening breeze. Around the hulls of the boats, and under the pilings, pools of diesel oil fouled the surface with viscous spectra. A gull was perched on the roof of our car when we returned. It left a memento trickling down the windshield as it flapped off.

We stopped at a supermarket and laid in a supply of fresh lettuce, green onions, tomatoes, a cucumber, a pound of lean ground beef, two six-packs of beer, tortillas, wedges of Monterey Jack and American cheddar, a bag of potatoes, spaghetti, tomato paste, sacks of brown and milled rice, dried pinto beans, flour and a package of oatmeal cookies. We have to take advantage of these trips into town to stock up on food. We've started a vegetable garden, but it doesn't produce much yet. Actually, it hasn't produced anything yet, mainly because I'm too lazy to tend it. And we don't have a refrigerator. (We don't have electricity or running water, either.)

Tonight would be a celebratory dinner. The doctor had told Sharon the baby had dropped. (She thought so.) He gave her two weeks. We bought an apple and a navel orange each, to chomp on the long haul home. Got to prevent scurvy. Outside of town we saw a vegetable stand. Sharon dickered with the lady and came away with a bag of fresh mushrooms and a pair of dead-ripe artichokes. Half price. I was surprised, because the locals usually squint into the distance distastefully when we pad up. Filthy, long-haired, immoral hippie parasites. I guess it was because Sharon looked so pregnant. I finished my apple, finished my orange, started in on the cookies. They were a foolish luxury, but I was hungry. We crept up through the canyons, the two spavined French horses whining Gallic protests all the way. I started caressing Sharon's stomach.

It was getting hotter as we inched sunward. The canvas roof was furled back. I could feel the bridge of my nose and my cheekbones beginning to redden. Sharon was dozing, her hand over mine on her swollen middle. Suddenly the horses developed an ominous borborygmus. I pulled off at a turnout to let the engine cool.

There was a spring-fed water fountain built into a low stone retaining wall in the lee of the turnout. We decided to have a drink. The water was clear and cold. When I unbent, my mustache and beard had soaked up about a pint. I snuck behind Sharon and sloshed a gelid kiss across her profile. She squealed and wrinkled her nose and twisted away. I chased her around the car, not running very hard because it was more fun to watch her waddle. Finally she dodged behind the wall and started up a narrow ravine. The foot was a dry stream bed, in this season only a tumble of crumbly rocks. The steep banks were choked with sage and scrub manzanita and poison oak. Shading the fountain and the mound of detritus at the base of the wall was a coast pine, tall and flat on top like a huge parasol. Sharon slowed as she picked her way higher. I bounded after her to give her a hand.

"Let's see where this goes," she panted.

"It doesn't go anywhere," I said. "Look out. You're going to fall and bust your bun." I grabbed a handful of dress just below her seat.

"Hey, come on, let go," she said. She squirmed and continued to claw at the dirt. "Don't be a poop. Come on!"

I craned my head and saw that the gully gouged its way out around a promontory, then appeared to switch back. About a hundred feet above us was a setback in the cliff face, a kind of shelf which we might be able to reach along this route. If we could, we'd have a great view of the coast, our own private niche in the wilderness, above the road and screened from it. I let her climb.

Sure enough, we came out on a small grassy flat. It was tipped slightly toward the sea, maybe twenty feet wide. There was a generous dusting of soft blue wildflowers.

"Hey, fantastic!" Sharon exclaimed.

We were both out of breath from the clamber. We flopped down on our backs in the cool grass. I hated to mash the flowers under me, but it couldn't be avoided. We lay there for a while, eyes closed against the red sun. Our fronts were broiling, our backs basting pleasantly in the earth's tepid vegetable juices. The armpits of my shirt were soaked. I sat up and peeled it off. In front of me shimmered maybe fifty miles of littoral—rocky inlets and coves sheltering inaccessible white sand beaches, abrupt cliffs rearing high above the surging water. Here and there, in the foothill basins, a cluster of trees stood in a brown pasture where tiny cattle, like toys on a train set, grazed over their shadows.

Around a point of land to the north the sky was smudged. I watched for a long time. I didn't even notice when Sharon sat up beside me. Not until her index finger probed the edge of my view.

"A ship," she murmured.

I nodded.

Far to the south, just barely discernible, a freighter with a generic black hull and white superstructure was beating its way toward us.

I lay back and cupped my hands behind my head. I squinted through my eyelashes at the sky. There wasn't a cloud. The sun glinted off the lashes prismatically. The slits of blue were bordered by rainbow lace. Tiny transparent squiggles, cellular-looking, floated across the blue. Dust particles? Amoebae?

I blinked. Commotion among the squiggles. Microscopic microcosm. Redundant? I closed my eyes and watched the colors change. Red to white to yellow to red again. The squiggles still visible if I looked for them. Placidly drifting above the chromatic abyss.

"What do you see when you turn out the light?" the Beatles inquire. Response: "I can't tell you but I know it's mine."

I was in an aqueous humor. Suddenly it occurred to me to turn on.

"Jesus, let's turn on," I said. "What a great place."

"Did you bring any stuff with you?"

"No. It's down in the car."

I scrambled to my feet. "I'll go get it."

I slid over the lip of the shelf and caromed down the ravine.
After making sure no traffic was approaching, I fished the Bull Durham pouch from its stash under the rear seat. When I hauled myself back beside Sharon she was stretched out on her side, idly coaxing upright the flowers I had flattened. She'd taken off her dress.

"Well, well, well," I said. Then, "Good idea."

I pulled down my pants, worked boots and wad of pants over' my feet, and squatted next to her. Full lotus. I took the packet of Zig-Zag papers from my shirt pocket and draped the shirt over my lap to catch any stray flakes of grass. I pasted two papers together, then cupped them between my fingers to form a trough. I shook a liberal mound of grass into the center. A seed had escaped my currying. I picked it out and swallowed it. Heh, heh. I spread the aromatic flakes evenly, then, with a few deft manipulations, rolled a firm fat joint. I licked the gum, crimped the ends. Appraised my handiwork. Stuck it between my lips. I gathered the crumbs from my shirt and returned them to the pouch. Pulled the drawstring, completing the lovely ritual. Next I am going to learn how to roll one one-handed. On horseback, at a full gallop. The Stoned Ranger: "Hi-Ho Silver, awa-a-a-a-a-ay!"

I lit up, inhaled deeply and passed the joint to Sharon. She sucked in a lungful, held her breath.

The stuff was good. On about my third puff I could suddenly feel the space growing between my brain and my cranium. Soon I was floating free inside my bone structure, scuttling deeper within, toward the core, like a homing testicle. Three more drags and my eyes were the only surface connection with the encephalic plexus. They throbbed and blinked and stung and bobbed like a slug's at the ends of their optic stalks. Absorbing data, transmitting raw images back to the central monitors. My face was numb. Sculpted meat. Useful only because it housed a mouth into which I could poke the joint. A monitor—that's what I was in the nautical sense: My head the vaguely decorative turret inside which the neurologic command huddled, receiving intelligence and issuing decisions. My body was just a hull. A gangling armored case for the ganglia. A locomotive platform, a bit deep-draft to be sure, but functional—studded with ports and hatches and booms and winches....

Sharon passed me the joint. Commands crackled out from the pons and the medulla oblongata. Made axons and dendrites hop to it with synaptic snaps:

"Bridge to diaphragm: Tense."

"Diaphragm aye."

"You got that, serratus? Lower those ribs."

"Aye, aye."

"Lung reports air expelled."

"Bridge aye. Stand by. Bridge to diaphragm: Relax."

"Diaphragm aye."

"Commence lowering."

"M. Serratus Posterior Superior hoisting ribs as directed, sir."

"Very well, MSPS, carry on. Excellent coordination."

"Lung reports chamber pressure falling fast."

"Bridge acknowledges."

"Message in from lips, sir. Joint breech-loaded and ready to fire."

"Ah. Commence firing. COMMENCE FIRING!"

"Cannabis smoke and air passing over tongue... now, sir! Tonsils report smoke contact closing that station at high speed. Confirmed by bronchi. All stations report green, sir! Smoke at ambient external pressure should be inflating depressurized lung sacs... stand by... stand by... MARK! Lung confirms. All alveoli readings at max capacity. Gas crossover going smoothly, sir. Signal from blood stream: 'Sighted THC, absorbed same.'"

"Good show, sparks. Alert all stations to clear for delivery ASAP. Has heart acknowledged?"

"Affirmative, sir. Bit jocular, though. Said: 'Here come de blood.'"

"Ah well, sparks, we have to make allowances for heart. Never gets any liberty, you know."

WHAM!

"HIT! HIT!"

"Bridge to organism: This is CNS speaking. I want to commend all hands for a tough job well done. I think we've earned a rest... so all non-vital stations may stand easy for three seconds. The smoking lamp is definitely lit. And I want you to know... I'm putting this crew in for the Congressional Medulla Honor."

After what seemed interminable amused—or more accurately, bemused—consideration, my mechanism merged with my personality again.

I undertook to convey that scenario from my pre-Nam Navy service to Sharon. I had a hard time, because my mind kept racing ahead of my mouth. Then it would abruptly pull up short and start listening to what the mouth was saying. And that was very confusing, because the mouth was always so laggard that the mind would have to retrace its steps and take the mouth by the hand, so to speak—the tongue, more appropriately—and figure out how to get them both back to the point where the mind had just been. Which by then, of course, it had itself forgotten!

And anyway, the path was pitted with conceptual divots, metaphors exactly like these which the headlong mind had torn up and over which it kept stumbling. And Sharon was laughing and I, too, thought my ideas were absolutely hilarious. So much so that I could scarcely squeeze out a complete sentence without succumbing to a fit of racking giggles. And Sharon offered her own embellishments, which were equally funny.

Before we were finished we were rolling in our naked skins on the grass, moaning and crying and hiccupping like victims of some fiendish Oriental tickle-torture. It was beautiful.

And then we both lay still for a while, catharted, minds calmly flashing. Ideas and images played the brain like Selected Short Subjects. I buried my chin in the grass and went on safari. Flushing from their camouflage the infinitesimal bug-ules that prowled these pampas. Behind a broad leaf lurked a terrifying specimen—rarely encountered at such close range. What a trophy he'd make! Look at the span of those serrated antennae, the brute power in those slavering mandibles, the malevolent courage in those glaring hemipterous eyes. Suddenly I forgot our relative sizes. In a panic I braced myself for the charge. But he gave ground, filament legs churning in commensurate panic as he scurried away into the twiggage. Phew.

But hark! "What's that rustling, bwana?" An ant plodded by. Huge and grim with obscure purpose. Perhaps he was an outrider, patrolling the bush for stray aphids from the herd. I let him pass without challenge. This was his territory.

Funny, I mused, that I should attribute human motives to the ant. I had likened the anonymous smaller insect to a beast. Was it a question of size? No, probably a question of society. The ant and I were both members of a complex social order. We were both expected to fill jobs, roles. And yet, at this moment, we confronted the world and each other alone. Without the distractive supports our societies offered. The existential condition. (I just thought that up.) Hell, maybe he was even a hippie ant, an outcast from the colony seeking formic truth in the recesses of a mind blown on fermented honeydew.

No, we were all alike: the ant, the microbug, the man. Knots of abstract intelligence pushing around utilitarian frames. We were differentiated—but we were undifferentiated too. Just three electrical charges playing out our brief circuitry. Sure, the capacities and the potentialities varied. But probably not the sophistication of the wiring. Has anyone diagrammed an ant's nervous system? To them I was big, to me they were small. Yet we were all divisible. I into bones and flesh... and then cells... and then molecules... and then atoms... and then protons, neutrons, electrons... and then... what? Our equations differed—but the materials, and the laws governing their reaction, were identical.

I turned my head to look at Sharon. She lay on her back nearby, stoned, breasts flaccid, occupied abdomen jutting firm as Gibraltar. Inside crouched the product of our coupling. One and one make three. One and one... and one? Wow. I mean, Sharon and I were distinct individuals, right? She was not I, I was not she. And I was not ant and ant was not I. And Sharon was not bug and bug was not Sharon. And....

But what about the baby? Was it Sharon now? Yes. And no. And where did we all stop? I mean, wow! Start dividing. Pretty soon all the walls disappeared. Where were our boundaries in the molecular sea? What had seemed my inviolable individuality was suddenly only an impermanent wash of carbon and nitrogen and hydrogen and oxygen and iodine and phosphorus and sodium and calcium and iron... percolating, interacting elements in a churning Mare Nostrum of carbon and nitrogen and hydrogen and oxygen and iodine and phosphorus and sodium and calcium and iron and ninety-four other ultimate stuffs. I—the material I—was only a vaguely charted eddy of proteins, carbohydrates, fats, enzymes, hormones, vitamins... a shifting pool of biochemical processes in a vast ocean of similar processes. Atoms mingling, adhering, disintegrating. And my human intelligence was no more than the product of all that friction. Peculiar because of minute variations in the chemical formulation, but not very peculiar, because the formulation was human. And when the component molecules ceased to vibrate to the necessary rhythms... bonds would lapse, cells would wither, ideational circuits would sputter out. One more electronic ego shorted, and not even a telltale whiff of ozone. "My" atoms spinning free, available for recombination. An infinitesimal ripple in the molecular tide.

Electron, proton, ion, cluster, chromosome, nucleus, cell, germ, mite, ant, lizard, cat, *man.*

And then elephant, whale, sequoia *gigantea...* mountain, continent, ocean, Earth. Volatile oblate spheroid, one of nine whirling about a fiery sun. Billions of similar energy systems exploding to the limits of cognition. Universe, finite. Among infinite universes.

Quasars. Antimatter.

Perhaps our science can only encompass the tiniest snippet of the continuum. Perhaps we are all just inhabitants of a flourine electron. And one of every nine electrons of each atom of flourine is an inhabited planet. Perhaps our solar system is right now under the scrutiny of some Brobdingnagian (raised to the nth power) electron microscope. While at the same time beeping intergalactic signals to some Lilliputian (reduced to the minus-nth power) radio telescope. The span of human history in a remote eyeblink. A spoke of static. Perhaps we are only one of an infinite series of ultimate particles and organisms and chemistries and physics, nestled into one another like a Chinese puzzle. Stored in a roomful of mirrors— matter on one side of the glass, antimatter on the other. And each in turn reflected. Infinity in infinite dimensions.

As I considered this cosmology my eyes screwed shut. Inward I plunged—down, down on the sucking mental undertow. I was like a diver experiencing rapture of the depths. I had maneuvered into the vortex, now I rode with it, steadily kicking and paddling—mesmerized by the elusive lure of the bottom.

Until suddenly I could see it. The idea had taken form. There: a glaring white pinprick far beneath the swirling colors of my inner vision. A pineal glow... the source, the nadir of the maelstrom. The beginning of infinity.

Man! I felt an overwhelming excitement. I was as near as I have ever been. If I could only reach it!

But I realized that once I did, I would have to die. Because the pressure at that ultimate depth would collapse me.

And yet I *could* reach it! I knew that. By harnessing all my electrical life energy... by concentrating, gradually shutting down all the motor and sensory branch circuits, switching off fingers, toes, then legs, then arms, then trunk, then taste, sight, hearing, smell... eliminating every coulomb of neurologic drain... and then boosting the resultant current, amplifying it, accelerating it, metering it very carefully until the voltage was crackling and rippling unrestrainable from the coils... and then suddenly shunting it through, into the core of the brain, in one single magnificent overpowering mental charge....

Yes! *I could!* I could propel myself into the central mystery! *Implode* with a final, searing, brilliant, blinding nuclear flash of... hm. Truth?

That would... that would... extinguish me. Impel me into some new, still, immaterial, eternal dimension. Maybe. Perhaps. But extinguish me. And I was hesitant. Not quite scared, no, but hesitant.

And then the nitrogen bubbles began to pop in my blood and my eustachian tubes ached and I leveled out. Trod water. Stared into the murky interior, curious.

I *could* do it. But, um, not today.

And then I shot to the surface with a laugh. Opened my eyes, sat up, picked a flower.

Sharon seemed to be asleep.

HEXAGRAM 2

K'UN

THE PASSIVE PRINCIPLE

*...Exalted indeed is the sublime
Passive Principle! Gladly it receives
the celestial force—the Creative
Principle—into itself, wherefrom all
things receive their birth....*

I had intended to tell her about my discovery, but she didn't promise much in the way of receptivity.

I crawled nearer, circling stealthily behind her head so my shadow wouldn't fall across her eyes. She was breathing regularly. I watched her breasts rise and rail. Roseate nipples tweaked by the breeze. Areolas slightly puffed, papillae raised but soft. Like nectar gumdrops. Sharon has beautiful breasts. She never wears a bra. Now, with the baby almost due, they had begun to swell. A wispy filigree or blood vessels surrounded the nipples. Surveying her body like this, from behind and above, I could see only promontories. Forehead, nose, cheeks, upper lip, teats—and commanding the range, the great dome of stomach, with its little convex saucer cap of distended navel. Except for one upthrust knee, all the topography beyond lay hidden. From her, too.

"I haven't seen my pussy in two months," she complained one morning.

I crawled down the length of her left arm, paused by her hip and discovered the lush copse flourishing in the vale between her thighs. Like stout Cortez, with a wild surmise. I laid the flower there, very gently.

"I hereby claim this territory in the name of...."

Her eyelids fluttered and she squinted at me.

"What...?"

"Nothing," I said. I backed off quickly on hands and knees, not wanting to disturb her. She closed her eyes again. The flower remained in place, blue petals on a tricornered field of brown.

Pot is funny. From a near delirium of mental involution I had abruptly unwound, like an overtaxed spring, into a state of awareness that was purely physical. Consciousness was all surface, skin. My own flesh responding to the beck of hers. The crawling had centered sensation in my dangling penis and scrotum. Now I sat back on my haunches, balls resting on thighs, and viewed Sharon. Letting the emanations from her feminine curves flow into my masculine angles. One growing more acute.

The sun radiated across my shoulders, back, chest, loins. Nature is sexual. Not only Sharon's nakedness—but the air, the sky, the grass, the sea, the muscles, sinews and fibers of my own body were giving me a hard-on.

I stood. I walked around the shelf. Preceded by my great, red, noble, glistening, straining, elongated cock. I felt the spongy earth beneath my toes. I felt the salt zephyrs in the cowlick over my forehead. I felt the air in my beard, in the tufts around my flat vestigial male nipples, in the pubic thatch across my lower abdomen, in the dank cleft between my buttocks. I felt my anus—a pursed-up rosebud. Cool rivulets of sweat rolled down my ribs. I grasped my penis in my fist, completing the narcissistic circuit.

My body, carefully clothed against fresh air and light for all but a few moments for most of its days, still reacts erotically to natural exposure. Perhaps that is as it should be. But I didn't want to jack off. I wanted to come like a lover into the universe.

I stood on the edge of the shelf facing the ocean, spread my arms, flexed my knee, rocked pelvis up, back, up, back, up, back—thrusting deep into the womb of the world. Pantomime. My bulbous purple glans gaped at the seam like a ripe acorn. Bulging with germinative power. I could imagine great oaks springing from my seed. I am Father of all things.

Below me the tiny freighter plowed through the endless ocean. Shipload of ants. Chained to routine. Confined in dim, foul, strait, clanking metal compartments. Resident servants to a rusting machine. Poor diminutive, diminished human beings. While I stood above them, large as life, Lord of the universe. Naked among the elements. Staff in hand...

"With this rod I command the seas to roll back."

No, that was unnatural.

"With this rod I command the seas to come, come, come."

And the seas obeyed. Deity is the art of the possible.

I ached to join in the tidal surge. My Godhead, I thought, is dual—penile as well as cerebral. Only when the two are united do we derive trinity: Orgasm, the Holy Spirit. As, on a broader plane, Idea and Flesh meld in Love. Which corresponds very nicely, you see, to the paradigm: God the Father—Idea—generates God the Son—Flesh—and their two-way love is the third—God the Holy Ghost. Isn't that how it's supposed to work, Augustine? Spermatozoa even look like ghosts. What a theologian I'd make!

But this was the subservience of idea to metaphor. A momentary distraction— mental masturbation. And at once all metaphysics drained into my prick again. I wanted to make love to Sharon, not the sky.

Dizzy, grinning, I stooped and gathered a handful of flowers.

Sharon still lay quietly behind me. A lumpy odalisque, receiving the sun. I squatted beside her and carefully threaded a stem into her silky pubic hair. Next to the first blossom— landscaping the *mons veneris.*

She flinched at my touch. Her eyelids popped open and she raised herself clumsily on her elbows.

"What are you doing?" she demanded.

"Nowt," I replied.

"Huh?" she said. She blinked. Her eyes were pink from the marijuana.

"Ah be pootin' flars in tha coont," I said. Whenever I am sexually aroused I slip into my Midlands dialect. I worked a third stem through the soft curls feathering her labia.

"Hey, that tickles!" she said.

"Tha's wha they allus says," I soothed her.

"Roger, phooey!" Sharon groaned, comprehending. "You nut! You don't even have the accent right, you know. It's atrocious."

"Ah canna he'p it. Tha's the way ah talks, do ye ken?"

"'He'p it,'" she laughed. "'Do ye ken?' What is that, some kind of weird cross between Stepin Fetchit and Robert Burns?"

"It's D.H. Lawrence!" I objected. "On Ilkley Moor, bart 'at?"

Sharon snorted again. She tossed her head to free the tangles in her blond hair. It fell long and straight behind her, the blunt ends brushing the matted grass where she had rested. A few damp strands stuck to her collarbone. She raised a hand to brush them away. She had been perspiring in the sun. Now it glinted in the tiny beads on her upper lip and the deep divide between her breasts and the fine brown hairs under her arm. I selected another flower from my bouquet. Sharon lay back, supporting her head on a fist. I leaned forward and set the flower in the dewy fleece of her armpit.

"Stop it!" she giggled. She shivered and dislodged the posy.

My hand had come to rest on her upstretched breast. Gently I pressed my fingers into its resilience. She had begun to sunburn, and the granular surface color flushed away around my fingertips. I felt the nipple tighten and rise under my palm. Its twin reflexively followed suit.

"Tha'rt some dish," I murmured.

"You gamekeepers are all alike," she sighed. "Trite."

"Trite?"

"The hoary flower bit."

"That's not trite," I protested, "it's symbolic You know, pistils and stamens…. Flowers are just straight-out sex

42

objects, right? Like a mandrill's ass. Brilliant colors to invite propagation."

"You're trying to get a bee to sting me down there, is that it?"

I laughed. "Come to think of it," I said, "I've read bees are color-blind."

Sharon had been watching my erection. Now she reached out and ran a tentative forefinger down my penis and around the taut scrotal folds. "Why don't you give me a little sting then yourself, Roger? I think I'm turning a brilliant color for you right now."

"Ho! Just what I had in mind," I nodded. "I'm not color-blind."

I brought my hand from her breast, over her ribs, up across her pregnant belly and down, slowly, into the musky declivity between her legs. Sharon licked her lips. She arched her back and stretched. Then she expelled her breath and relaxed, turning on her side and drawing her legs up compliantly. Now they were splayed, giving me access to the pink vulval recesses. I touched her juice. With a moistened finger I sought her clitoris. She shivered again and closed her eyes. I discarded my bouquet. I settled. alongside her, full length, my genitals biting hard into the flesh of her flank. Her hand crept between us, found my dick and clenched around it. I kissed her. Our teeth clacked and she winced. And then her tongue probed deep into my mouth, hot, curled, wet, rasping across my glossal buds, eagerly darting into dental and gingival crannies as she tasted for oral secrets. Just as my hand palpated her genital privacies. Her breathing quickened. I could feel the air in my lungs being sucked into hers. And hers damply inflating mine. Our salivas—and now our very life energies—commingled. Carbon dioxide, water, spent cell and tissue fragments interflowing, shared. Legs and arms twined—the precoital love-knot. Her breasts, soft, plump, pinioned, pillowed my chest. I drew away, slithered down and kissed her nipples. Firm, salient, knurled. Lightly crusted with colostrum. She knotted my hair and squirmed.

"Will you... nurse me like that... when the baby comes?"

"Yes. I want to taste your milk."

She smiled.

"One spigot for me, one for the baby at feeding time."

"Poor kid. He'll be undernourished. While his father gets fatter and fatter."

She clasped my face tighter into her bosom. "That's okay." She purred as my teeth dryly worried her stimulated pap.

I worked myself lower. I licked the salty liquor from the creases where breasts meet torso. Slicked the fine down across the ridges of her ribs. Tongued the evolute navel. I have a compulsion to ingest. Or at least taste. Corroborate the visual and tactile with the olfactory and gustatory. Or maybe it's just my feeble male attempt to intussuscept the female. Sharon— succulent momsicle.

With cheeks and lips I traced the swollen lineaments of her womb. Asymmetric bulges mapping fetal attitudes. Beneath me, only inches away, lolled our baby. Ankles crossed... here? Knees up... here? Thumb, perhaps here... in maw. Alive and well, thank you, but not yet accepting invitations. Comfortably, lazily swishing in its amniotic bath. Wrinkled, sightless, upside down. Shedding its brindle nap. Recapitulating phylogeny. While I recapitulated philogyny.

I listened for the heartbeat. All I heard was the gurgle of Sharon's stomach and the stroke of her blood. Ebb and flow— engorging the *glans clitoridis*. I followed its course. Down, where the fine white hairs on her abdomen met and darkened in a bisecting line. Down to a pair of tiny brown moles. Two full stops in obedience to physical punctuation. Then on to the ultimate bloom of piedmontane foliage. In its benign shade the skin was milky, inviting the mouth. I kissed her cunt. Swell and dip—soft bifurcated dip. And groin incurves, parchment thin. Lightly blued with pulsing veins.

My beard and mustache tangled in the whorls of her pubic beard. My insidious tongue lapped at the portals of *rima pudendi*. "The cleft of shames." Latin betrays some atavistic hangups. But I am an unrestrained linguist. Seeking slake in all Sharon's fluids. Tart and tepid. Saline, this. Fragrant. Nutlike. My lips closed around the flavoring nut. Shifted it rhythmically. Sharon's pelvis jerked. Muscles twitched spasmodically. She moaned and drew my head away. Brought my mouth once again to hers. Panted kisses, face suffused. Neck and chest mottled, her sweating body tensed against mine. My knee between her thighs. Her vulva wet and clinging. I kissed her swollen lips, her fragile eyelids, her temples, her ears. Filled the waxen mazes with the roar of my sounding tongue.

Suddenly she lurched away, pushed me back and bent over me. Hunched and wrinkled around her beachball belly. Breasts bovine, pendulous. Her hair falling forward. Modest drape. Tingling ringlets cascading on my abdomen. My balls turning to jelly as she sized my dilated foreskin. Lipskin pursed around unmelting popsicle. Her tongue licked away the viscid beads from my penis tip. Tested, tentative. Then swallowed. Mouth gulping, juicing, sliding. Teeth nipping, teasing. Soul suck. I grappled with her cunt. Vicious. We exchanged ecstatic pains. And then we were together again. Locked, rolling, gasping.

"Come into me now."

"Mm. Mm. I love you."

"Love... you."

Careful not to squunch pregnant womb. I could still do her from the front. I spread her legs, knelt between. Cradled buttocks. Groped for gape. Her fingers guided. Into vagina. In, sliding, liquid glide. Up, deep, hilted. *Pubes* grinding. In, out, in. Liquid, lymphoid internal caresses. Spongy grip focussing sense. Bellies sweating, squeaking, rubbing. My knees slewing on the slippery grass. Her ankles crossed behind my butt.

Kicking me deeper on every stroke. Apex of strokes a cervical thump. And flatulent blaps as I mashed her breasts flat. Her face a grimace as my root reamed home. Innards flaming, juices sluicing. Hot breath panting. Rhythm rising. Coming, coming. Together now? Pressure mounting, our loins both burning. Working, grunting, swelling, seeping, loving, fucking. The spirit physique. My love for Sharon a glandular secretion. Flooding now. I couldn't stop it.

"I'm going to come."

"Oh!" she breathed. "Oh!"

She lurched. Shuddered, cried out. And I exploded. Hot sperm bursting through blazing breach. Senses swirled in cataclysm. Essential current rushing to her. And Sharon hurled limp on responsive waves. Orgasm, climax. My mind washed free. Once again whirled toward the central void. Flushed deep inside by the vacuum of spurting. Once again spun toward the glimmering gap. The pineal gash in the fabric of life. Coming... keep coming! I would pump myself through. Through into Sharon—and then both beyond. Sexual union: one together. Inside OUT!

Inside... out. But....

It was over.

And we lay, inertly coupled, drained, exhausted. The spasms subsiding slowly. Heart rates decelerating. Now and then a faint, reminiscent wiggle. Kisses and sighs. Light lip brushes, mumbled endearments. My arm was cramped. I shifted it. She coughed and rearranged her legs. I propped myself on an elbow, peeled inhaled blond strands from my nose and tongue. She blinked a stray eyelash from the corner of her lid.

"I love you," I said. "You're one great lay."

She smiled and squeezed her vaginal muscles playfully. My penis was wilting. Soft sausage stuffing. Sore and spent. Like the poor, ill-fated, lost spermatozoa I'd just evicted. Churning doggedly, futilely upstream. Seeking the legendary

46

Golden Ovum. *El Dorhuevo.* The Treasure of Sierra Madre. They would die valiantly, broken, never having fulfilled their quest. Like trillions before them. Except for one plucky devil, mated and mitosed. The great-great-great-great-great-great-and-so-on-grandfather of the gestating organism beneath me.

I gave it a mushy prod. Not that it hadn't had enough already. Probably be born with some kind of complex. And covered with bruises.

No, no. We'd been assured sex was okay.

I withdrew from Sharon. A gobbet of semen oozed out with me. We cuddled, sweaty and sticky, our sexes glazing in the sun.

HEXAGRAM 3

CHUN

DIFFICULTY

...This hexagram symbolizes lightning spewed forth by the clouds—difficulty prevails! The Superior Man busies himself setting things in order....

We'd dozed off.

When we roused ourselves the afternoon was over. The sun was low in the northwestern sky and the fog had started back in. The underside or the bank was flat and leaden, and the coastline beneath it was already in twilight. But the sky above was a deep clear blue and the fog tops, at our level, were like cotton candy—all back-lighted orange swirls and puffs and hummocks. It made you wish you could dive in and wallow on the soft billows.

I was hungry as a bastard—God, I was hungry! It was the pot, of course. We scrambled up and put on our clothes. We were both pretty sunburned. The backs of my knees and my shoulders and the small or my back were beet red. Not to mention my penis which, in addition, was caked stiff with crystalline come. Sharon said her nipples were sore.

We picked our way down the ravine, me in front so she'd have something to lean on. Her feet skidded out from under her once, and she sat down. I kept her from falling too hard. At the car I tucked the marijuana out or sight. We'd had a good trip, and now felt very placid and sated. Except I was famished. While I struggled to convince the French engine it ought to turn over, I ate two cookies—slowly, relishing their rough oatmeal texture and subtle tang. But I wanted to preserve this heightened appreciation for supper. So— exercising mighty restraint—I held my snack to two. Finally we got underway. The fog was just rolling over the clearing as we churred up to the cabin.

We washed ourselves at the pump, Sharon squatting with her skirts tucked under her armpits, slapping handfuls of water between her legs. The sight gave me another crotch-bulge. But we both agreed our appetites were really more visceral than venereal now. Sharon went inside to make rice and the artichokes. I unloaded the groceries from the car. Then I got a bucket, a knife and a sheet of old newspaper and set about cleaning the squid. It was going to be a weird meal. I peeled off the membranes, removed the cartilaginous spines, discarded the innards and ink sacs. (If you were a castaway, I mused, you could keep a journal by cleverly utilizing the ink and quill-like backbones of squid. Though catching them might present something of a problem. I tried to work out a pun on "squid" and "squib." Unsuccessfully.) I popped out the beaks and eyes and sliced the hoods into quarter-inch rings. There were eight squid, each about eight inches long. When I was finished I took my wet mound of rings and tentacle rosettes into the kitchen. Sharon had lit a candle, although there was still plenty of light filtering in through the dirty window. She was standing over the stove, wreaths of steam boiling up around her from the artichoke pot. Her face was flushed, her hair tucked back behind her ears. Careless lovelocks straggled damply down her cheeks. She looked thoughtful. I set my newssheet platter on the table.

"Okay, these are all clean and cut up. You want me to make the batter?"

"No, I'll do it."

"I might as well," I said. I walked over, leaned around her and began to sort through the bags piled into the shadowy corner beside the stove. I was looking for the flour sack. "Where'd you move...?"

"Guess what, Roger."

"...The flour. I put it right.... What?" I glanced up at her. She was smiling at me crookedly.

"Guess what. I've just had two labor pains."

It took me a second to absorb what she'd said. I straightened and backed away. "What?"

"Yeah." She laughed, turning to lean her hip against the

oven door handle. The words started tumbling out, crowding each other like awakening firemen. "The first one was right after I came in. Just this sort of very weak little backache, you know... except... and I wouldn't even have noticed it except it kept getting sharper and sharper, you know, building up, like somebody was digging down underneath my spine with a trowel, twisting and twisting in deeper. And then the second one came just a few minutes ago." The proud, slightly embarrassed, excited smile flashed again. "It felt the same way."

"Yeah?" I grinned back. "How long'd they last?"

"Oh, maybe about thirty seconds or so."

We chuckled in chorus.

"How far apart were they?" I asked.

"I don't know. I guess about fifteen minutes probably."

"Gee, we ought to have a clock. I need a watch."

"Well, you can tell when they get closer and closer."

"Yeah." I stared at the sacks. "Of course, they could be false labor too, of course."

"Oh sure. That's probably what they are," she agreed. "Probably just my cervical muscles limbering up, stretching and all, the way they say? But it's neat anyway. My first contractions. Maybe it'll be sooner than two weeks. You think?"

I laughed. "I don't know. Could be."

Sharon turned back to the stove, once more thoughtful. "They really didn't hurt that much either. You know?"

I had resumed rooting among the sacks. "I told you they wouldn't," I said. I'd always tried to be upbeat. Reassuring.

Sharon finally pointed me to the flour—it was under the table—and I scooped some into the bag which held the artichokes. Then I pounded up a few old hard slices of sourdough French bread and scraped the crumbs into the bag. I sprinkled in a couple of pinches of garlic salt, dropped a handful of squid rings into the mixture and shook the bag.

"Hey," I said, "you should have put the oil on."

Sharon nodded and went to get another pot from the hook by the window. She set it on the burner and was just reaching up for the salad oil from the shelf over the stove when I heard her inhale sharply. I looked around and saw her with her hand upstretched, the other clutching the edge of the stove. She was standing motionless, frozen.

"What's the matter?" I blurted. I was alarmed but, pretty sure what the matter was, I sternly tamped my alarm.

Sharon didn't say anything for a second. Then she exhaled, continued her reach for the bottle, grasped it and brought it down. She unscrewed the cap. "There was another one," she grinned.

"Hm," I said.

Sharon filled the pot with oil and lit the burner.

"They seem fairly regular, don't they?"

Sharon chuckled. "Yep."

"Of course, that's only three."

"Oh, even if this is really labor, Roger, I don't expect much is going to happen for a long, long time."

"No, I know. But it's hardly going to go on for two more weeks...."

"Well, it could, actually. If this is just false labor."

"Of *course* it could *then,* for Christ's sake! Jesus! What I'm trying to get at is whether...!"

I realized my voice was rising angrily. I was probably more nervous than Sharon. I took a breath and slowed down. Adopted an even tone.

"Okay. Excuse me. I'm getting too worked up there. What I mean... I just was trying to figure out whether this was really labor starting or not. And I guess there's no way you can tell except to wait. So okay. Let's eat dinner."

Sharon nodded coolly.

We deep-fried the squid in oil—a messy business that I conducted.

You gingerly pop in a few breadcrumb-and-flour-coated rings and then hastily clamp a lid over the pot to contain the oil, which has bubbled and crackled up violently. After about thirty seconds you scoop out the cooked products. If you're lucky, you don't start a grease fire in the process. I was lucky. While the golden hooplets drained on a fresh sheet of paper, Sharon went outside and got our precious stick of butter from the cold-water tub under the house. She melted some and then served up the rice and artichokes. She had also brought in two cold beers. We ate at the kitchen table by candlelight. It was cozy. The fog had turned the evening chilly. The window was steamy from the kitchen warmth. We ate with our fingers, peeling off the artichoke leaves and dipping them into the melted butter, helping ourelves to squid slices from the central heap on the newspaper. Sharon doesn't like the tentacle portions, which curl up to look like big brown tarantulas. I love them. Chewy, salty and slightly garlicked. On the other hand, I'm not so fond of artichoke. But I was ravenous, and tonight it tasted delicious. The salty flavor of the squid was mitigated by the moist blandness of the rice. Sharon cooks it Japanese style. And we washed everything down with long drafts of beer from the beaded cans. Um-yummy! I still had my ap-pot-tite. So, apparently, did Sharon. We were both so busy biting and masticating and salivating and swallowing and licking our chops that we didn't have much time left over for conversation. Finally, though, the platter was bare. The table was littered with curled, tooth-scarred green leaves, a grease-stained sheet of newspaper, a speckling of batter crumbs, a couple of rattling cans, a dish of congealed butter and two smeary white plates. With a guttering candle for a centerpiece. I pushed back my chair and patted my glowing stomach.

"That, I am constrained to announce, was a regal repast," I declared. "I eschew false modesty. My skill with a squid surely rivals the most inspired creations of M'sieu Escoffier."

"I don't mean to escoff," Sharon jibed, "but pardon me while I throw up. Bleaaach!"

"Throw up! Don't you know the gentle gustatory gladdenance and... um, delicate, uh, ventral... uh... soothingness... of my captivating cookery would not permit it? Heh,heh, heh. Throw up, indeed."

"You kind of stumbled there, didn't you, baby? 'Soothingness....' A poetic genius ought to be able to do better than that."

"Snort," I snorted. "My wits have been dulled... microscopically... by the instomachation of great quantities of ambrosial provender."

"So that's where your wits reside."

"Look at this table!" I tacked. I swept my hand before me. "This reminds me of one of the more depraved excesses of Franz Hals or Jan Steen or somebody. And you sitting across there, fat and flushed... and leering, and mountainously preggers. Right out of one of those Flemish booze scenes! You ought to be ashamed of yourself."

Sharon's riposte was to give me the finger.

"Hey!" I exclaimed. I sat forward, abruptly earnest. "What about the pains?"

Sharon's expression immediately resolved into solemnity. She shrugged.

"You haven't had any more?"

"Nope. Not since we started eating."

"That's way more than fifteen or twenty minutes, then, isn't it?"

"Oh yeah."

"Then they *were* just false labor."

"Mm. Braxton-Hicks. I guess. I said that's all it probably was."

"Yeah."

We sat silent for a moment. In a way I was disappointed. And in a way not. I mean, why rush it?

"Well," I said finally, pushing myself up with the flat of my hand, "let's clear this mess off and retire to the drawing room."

"Okay."

"Hey, baby," I cooed. I circled the table and put my arm around her. I squeezed. "Hey, don't worry about it. Two weeks'll go by just like that." I snapped my fingers. "Right?"

Sharon's head bobbed unenthusiastically.

"Hell, you're probably right," I said. "It'll probably be sooner than that now. Anyway, you know, that's only a rough guess."

"Oh, is it, Roger?" she replied. "Gee. I thought it was the word of God."

Even her sarcasm trailed away disconsolately. She slumped in the chair, mouth drawn down and sunk in a pile of chins.

"The problem is," she snapped, "I want to get it over with right now! I'm tired of being... all puffed up. Lugging this big foreign object around in my middle. I want to be thin again. And be able to stoop down. And be able to drop acid. I want to stop being tired all the time. I want to be able to do what I want to do... without having this damn parasite...." She flicked herself angrily with a finger. "...Slowing me down and sucking up all my energy and everything! *That's* why I'm impatient."

"I know."

"The hell you do! *You're* not the one who used to get up and *vomit* every damn morning for three months! And you're not the one who has to go to the *bathroom* every four-and-a-half minutes! And you're not the one who has to stop eating and go on a diet and *lose* twenty pounds when this thing is all over. And you're not the one who has to have some squalling infant tugging and munching at your boobies every couple of hours all day and all night, whenever. And...."

"I know. You're right," I agreed. *"Touché."*

"Hell!"

Sharon sighed loudly. The flanges of her nose were red. Even pregnant, though, she is not given easily to tears. She stirred and straightened in her chair. I tried to think of more soothing words. I couldn't. I decided a discreet withdrawal would be the soundest tactic. I gave her a pat and started to back off.

"I'm sorry, Roger," Sharon blurted. She reached around and caught me by the hand. "I shouldn't be feeling so damn selfish and sorry for myself."

"Sure you should."

"No I shouldn't. Especially when you're just trying to be nice. And I mean anyway it's not true. I'm exaggerating. The main reason I'm impatient is because I'm all excited about giving birth. Aren't you?"

"Well ... sure." *Giving birth.* The phrase, aloud, sounded pompous.

"I mean, isn't it neat? My first baby! My first child. Our child. It's almost hard to believe. Coming right out of me, just out of my own body. A real, live, little tiny human being."

She laughed. "To have it happen. You know? It's been nine months, and now I'm ready for it."

"Yeah," I nodded. "Only maybe the other half of that act isn't quite as ready yet as you are. Ever think of that?"

"Mm. Well. I sure wish it would hurry up."

"If it's any constellation, baby, so do I."

"I suppose," she said after a beat, "that's what you call your planet parenthood."

I gave her the finger. Nonsense had been restored.

While Sharon made passes at ordering the kitchen, I gathered up the garbage and took it outside.

We store it in a box in a corner of the shed that houses

her pottery wheel. She hasn't been doing much work lately. Every so often, when the box starts to reek, I haul the whole mess away to a dumping area. Meanwhile we have to keep our swill out of the reach of raccoons. The night was cool and there were rents in the fog through which I could see icy stars overhead. Inside the shed, where it's pitch dark, I stubbed my toe against a sharp edge of Sharon's kickwheel. I hopped around and cursed and topped off my anger by just flinging the garbage bundle in the general direction of the box. I heard it splat against the wall and then something else fell and broke with a dull clayey thud. One of Sharon's drying pieces, no doubt. Shit. Chastened, I forgot my pain and stumbled back into the night air. I decided I'd keep quiet until I could survey the damage in the morning. I hoped it wasn't anything especially original. Mostly she just makes good utilitarian, saleable bowls and cups and saucers and teapots. But she does have flair. I might have destroyed some precious brainchild.

Because of my guilty conscience, I took a little detour walk around the clearing. A eucalyptus grove is always noisy, with leaves and seedpods and shreds of bark and even an occasional branch chattering to earth. But at the apex of my stroll, right on the verge of the trees, I was startled by a sudden loud thrashing in the underbrush. The sound diminished as whatever I had flushed—probably a deer—scurried deeper into the woods. I wished I'd carried a flashlight. We often surprise—or are surprised by—deer foraging almost up to our steps. Even so, the thrill of seeing them has not yet worn off.

As I turned and started back toward the house, a three-quarters moon flashed through the drifting fog. Our cabin is a drab, grey, sagging, paintless collision of rhombic planes resting skewed on twelve strategic cinder blocks. It's an abandoned tenant's shack we are allowed to occupy rent-free by a painter friend whose San Francisco uncle owns this whole scraggly ranch. (He is patiently waiting for the nearest cities to spread and render the unkempt land subdividable.) But in the fleeting silver light it took on an eerie dignity. Dignity, no doubt, because it was eerie: the stature conferred by fiction. The shack soaked up and refracted associations from Steinbeck and Thoreau and Faulkner and Alfred Hitchcock. And I perceived myself in its terms. I was the guy, say, photographed in *LIFE*, maybe, occupying this rural hovel. A bearded recluse with his hippie woman—Sharon's shadow had passed across the candlelit window—resolutely scorning all the *frou-frou* of civilization, determinedly celebrating the joys of rusticity according to the great American transcendentalist tradition. And I was pleased to see myself shuffling around the edges of that definition. And then the moon faded back behind the fog.

When I went inside I found Sharon humming at the kitchen table. She had a big lump of damp clay in front of her and was messing around with experimental hand-built forms.

"I just scared a deer or something out there," I said.

"Mm."

"The moon came out for a minute. This place really looks cool in the moonlight."

She smiled. She was busy shaping a flattened strip into a pinchpot.

"Anything happening?" I asked.

She knew what I meant. She shook her head.

I was kind of relieved. I wandered into the other room. The broken whatever still had me a bit worried. I lit a fat Mexican candle and lay on my back on the mattress. For a while I watched the shadows dance on the ceiling. A cobweb in the corner above me undulated in time to Sharon's humming. Uncanny. I got up and got a stick of incense—sandalwood— and lit it in the candle flame. I stuck it in the ceramic holder Sharon had made. Then I went back and watched the incense smoke graph air currents in the room.

When we first moved out here I used to go batty at

night. I couldn't read by candlelight, there was no television, no movie theaters or friends within range and all the radio stations we could pull in before Sharon's transistor batteries wore out sounded the way Daguerreotypes look. I had none of the usual distractions to get outside my mind. Now, though, after five months, I can just lounge around and placidly bubble up idle thoughts for hours. Some progress, huh?

But I guess, really, it's a psychic improvement to be able to groove on one's plain, unshaped, unamplified, unelectrified environment. Sometimes I think it's electric light—and ramifications—that cause modern man to be so screwed up. Constant jamming and jangling of natural Brownian movement. I know, it's not an original hypothesis. And anyway, mankind was screwed up long before there was a tungsten bulb. It's just that most of the damage had to be crammed into the daylight hours. Only eccentric troublemakers like philosophers and alchemists and poets sat up at night peering dimly over sheets of foolscap. Probably that's what's wrong with the Twentieth Century. The *hoi polloi* can entertain night-thoughts now too. And act on them. Late night TV as the ultimate expression of Dread. At one a.m. the Nielsen households are out of rhythm with the universe.

I decided to smoke another joint. I used to turn on almost every night. Now it's more occasional. I rolled a stick from the stuff in the ceramic jar. I am a simple pothead. No foil-lined corncob pipes or *creme de menthe*-cooled *nargilehs* for me.

"Hey, Sharon," I called. "I'm going to toke up again. Want to join me?"

"No thanks. I'm otherwise occupied."

"'Kay."

I smoked. Sharon had made a ceramic lantern top to fit over the candleholder. I put it on. It was perforated so that, as the flame flickered, shifting patterns were projected on the ceiling. A mini-light show. I lay back digging that for a long time. Really getting into it. After a while I noticed that the incense stick had burned down. I hauled myself up and got a replacement. My movements were like a swimmer's. I was buoyed several feet off the floor by the heavier medium of darkness that filled the room. When I ignited the new incense stick I was instantly mesmerized by its glowing red tip. And fine, spiraling twin contrails of blue smoke. First they would rise straight, and then suddenly contort. Sinuous accordion pleats, twisting finally into a double helix. God damn you, Watson and Crick! See, I could have demonstrated that answer too! If only I'd known the problem. Win a noble prize. I am understandably incensed. Deoxyribonucleic acid. It has now become clear that we are all acidheads. *Ergo* ergot. Lysergic acid diethylamide. LSD: skeleton key. Springs the locks on the peptide chains. Admits us once again to the prezygotic treasury. Where all cellular possibilities are stored. My templates disassembled. Reduced to ultimate potentiality. I can be a tree, a flower, a scampering Dalmatian. A scuttling salamander on a sunny log. Because DNA goes all the way. I *am* what I conceive—no distinctions, no dichotomies. When a little pHantasy pHudge has neutralized my logical alkalinity.

God, I thought, as soon as Sharon has unburdened herself we've got to trip out again.

I rolled the incense stick between my thumb and forefinger. The burning ember jogged. Pot ideation seeped away in smoke. I focused on the fiery spot. Carved my name with it into the darkness. Then I blew out the candle so I could see the light trail better. Making abstract expressionist neon zooms and swoops and arabesques. Las Vegas of the mind-eye lag. Giant Steinberg signatures.

I lit another stick. Waved both arms. I lay on the mattress and tried a supine Leonard Bernstein. Conducting a suddenly welling and very distinct interior Mozart *Eine Kleine Nachtmusik*. Full-tone stereo—switching at will between my left and right acoustic labyrinths. Surprised Bernstein hasn't yet thought of mounting the podium with blazing batons. I laughed as I developed that scene.

After a while the first stick burned out. And my arms got tired. I tried propping the one that was left in my navel. The wooden point hurt. I heard Sharon go outside. She must have been gone for a long time. I didn't hear her come back in.

HEXAGRAM 4

MÊNG

IMMATURITY,
UNCULTIVATED GROWTH

*...At the foot of the mountain lies
a dangerous abyss. To abide where
danger lurks is youthful folly. Yet such
rashness may bring good fortune—
fortune to be utilized when the
moment comes....
This hexagram suggests stubbornness
(the upper trigram) issuing from
the softness of the womb (the lower
trigram)....*

I woke up to a knee sporadically jabbing my hip.

I hate that. But it took me a while to decide it wasn't just another unpleasant episode in my kaleidoscopic dreams. I had slipped imperceptibly into a shallow, turbulent drowse. The egress was almost as subtle. Apparently my eyes had flapped open some time ago. The moonlight was angling in through the window, giving the room the same nacreous surrealism as my dreams—a kind of low-resolution chiaroscuro suitable to almost any level of consciousness.

Until I got another poke. That settled the matter. I was awake, in my most persistent and congruent frame of psychic reference. And Sharon was thrashing on the mattress next to me.

Grumpily I rolled out of range of her bones. In the process I caught a glimpse of her face. It was contorted. She was lying on her side, toward me, doubled up. There was something about those details that was supposed to mean something. But my brain was too full of sand for the gear-teeth to mesh.

Sharon wriggled a little and I watched, far away, up close. And then she seemed to relax. I heard her breathe out and swallow. She fluffed the pillow under her cheek and straightened her legs. And belatedly my thought-wheels engaged.

"Hey. What's the matter?" I whispered.

"Mp." She didn't open her eyes.

"Huh?"

"Nothing."

"Okay." I was satisfied.

"The pains started up again."

"Mm." I noticed that I was clothed and lying on top of

the blankets. My bare feet were numb. I raised myself on an elbow and unzipped my pants.

"Hey," I said, suddenly realizing what I had been told. "They did?"

"Mm-hm."

"When?"

"About an hour ago I guess."

"How long have I been asleep?"

"A couple of hours."

"Hm!" I pulled off the pants, tugged my shirt over my head and got under the blankets. The mattress ticking, except where I had been lying, was cold. I snuggled up against Sharon.

"Hey!" she snapped. "Your feet are freezing!" She kicked me away.

I didn't pursue her. Because all at once, as I thought about what she had said, I was afraid of her. Or anyway, of her distended body. It was doing strange internal parturient things—things I was leery of messing up if I prodded her in the wrong place. Things I wasn't so sure I wanted to be snuggling up against anyway.

"How many have you had?" I asked. "Are they regular?"

"Mm-hm. Pretty. I've had... mm, let's see... five."

"Gee!"

"They last about half a minute, I'd guess. About every fifteen minutes. Nothing to worry about yet."

"No," I agreed. I started worrying.

"But you know what else?"

"What?"

"When I went to the bathroom, I had a bloody show."

"Yeah?" Now I was really worrying.

"Mm-hm. Although I couldn't really tell how much it was because it was too dark. But there was quite a bit on the toilet paper when I wiped myself."

"You could see that."

"Mm-hm."

I tried to remember the full implications. Sharon was catching me off guard. I don't believe in a lot of unnecessary anticipation, and so I had been dilatory in my homework. This would have been just about the point, with a comfortable two weeks to go, when I would have launched into a serious, leisurely study of the subject of childbirth. But Sharon's impatience—and it was beginning to look as though it would produce a *fait accompli*—threatened to sabotage me. Unless I did some pretty quick brushing up right then and there.

Not that I wasn't reasonably ready. But I wanted to be readier. On the other hand, I couldn't do anything that might shake Sharon's confidence. Had to be casual. Furtive.

I lay still for a while, waiting to see if she'd offer any more but not encouraging it. I pretended I had drifted back into an unconcerned snooze. She was quiet too. After what seemed an adequate lapse I crept stealthily out from under the blankets.

"Where are you going?" she asked. Her voice had that clear wakeful edge.

"Take a piss," I whispered, very softly and, I hoped, very soporifically.

"I'm sorry I woke you up," she said.

"You didn't," I whispered. "Go to sleep."

"I'll try. Every time I do I have another pain."

"Well, try to sleep between them," I counseled. "You'll need plenty of rest."

"Mm. I know."

"I may stay up for a bit. I got too much sleep this afternoon."

"Me too," she said.

"No you didn't." I crawled back and kissed her below the ear. "Maybe the pains'll go away. And if they don't, and this is the beginning... you know... it'll be all the harder to rest up later. Right?"

"Mm. I guess."

"So just relax. I'll be back in a bit."

I grabbed my pants and shirt and padded away into the kitchen. I stepped outside, naked, and squeezed off a sizzling jet of urine under the house. So as not to be a liar. My breath clouded and my dick shriveled to about half and inch in length. I was hopping with horripilation. I scampered back inside and swathed my gooseflesh in clothing. Then I lit a candle and tiptoed around the bedroom again looking for our paperback manual on childbearing. I finally located it under the *I Ching*. I settled down at the kitchen table and, first or all, looked up "show" in the index.

"Intermittent contractions of the uterus," I read, "known as Hicks' sign or Braxton Hicks contractions after the English gynecologist John Braxton Hicks (1823-1897), occur throughout the pregnancy beginning sometime after the third month. Ordinarily they are painless, but in later months they may become painful and occasionally are difficult to distinguish from true labor. This is more often the case with multipara than primipara. However, change of position often stops such 'false' labor contractions. Another distinguishing feature of true labor pains is that they are rhythmic, and gradually increase in frequency and intensity. Moreover, the pains of true labor are ordinarily accompanied by a moderate show of blood, indicating dilation of the cervix and discharge of the mucous plug which has sealed the mouth of the womb during pregnancy. 'Show,' although it may precede true labor by a day or more, never occurs during false labor. (Nevertheless, it must be distinguished from abnormal, undiluted bleeding, which may occur at any time and should be regarded as a serious danger signal.)"

So. Wow.

I got up, hunted around for the oatmeal cookies, stuck one in my mouth and carried an extra back to the table. I reread the paragraph. My eyes were watery and their focus unsteady. My pulse was kind of pumping too. Because, according to this,

Sharon was definitely in labor. Bloody good show! For her, if not for me. But it sure did induce a sense of urgency.

I rolled myself a cigarette, nibbled nervously at the cookies and, skimming where possible, bulled through six detailed chapters on the stages of labor, pain relief, delivery, when to go to the hospital, modern obstetrical practices, complications—including such esoteric, and scary, possibilities as the use of forceps, version, breech extraction and cesarean section. A lot of the stuff didn't seem to apply. So I think I got a firm enough grip on what did. Firm as possible when you're coming down off a pot high and a couple of hours' sleep, it's the middle of the night and you've got one ear tuned for the occasional grunt wafting out of your pregnant old lady's bedroom door. When I figured I'd milked as much as I was going to get out of the book, I scissored my legs down from the tabletop, blew out the candle and went to see if it was feasible to catch a little more shuteye. Things were going to start popping soon enough.

I perched on the edge of the mattress and removed my pants. If worse came to worst, I mused, at least I should be able to get a job as a quick-change artist. Sharon had her back to me. She seemed unnaturally still. I got the idea she was awake but trying not to scare off sleep by acknowledging her wakefulness. I took off my shirt and edged under the blankets. I figured if she didn't say anything it would be all right for me to black out.

Which I was proceeding to do—because she didn't— when she flung away her covers and bustled over my lifeless form.

"Huh? What's up?" I bleated, quickly restored to life.

"Bathroom."

It was one of those cryptic midnight monosyllables designed to appease a sleeper without actually stirring him to thought. But naturally my mind had to creak into action to supply the elided grammar. Anyway, I could hardly ignore the tremors rocking me. I blinked the gunk out of my eyes and watched her disappear through the door. Moonlit silver nude, compact buttocks rolling like fine ball-bearings. I heard the backdoor slam, heard her footsteps fade in the direction of the crapper. Pretty soon she came back.

"*Jesus!* It's freezing!" she hissed as she dashed for the blankets. She hugged herself tight above her pear-shaped belly. Again her skin gleamed fish-silver except for the shadowy fuzz sprouting triangularly under the pear. Her breasts swung and jounced in her arms, the nipples furled up hard like a couple of pink erasers. She dived into the warmth on my side, forcing me to give way. I slid toward the wall. Her half of the mattress had cooled in her absence.

"Thanks a lot," I muttered, searching for residual pools of body heat. "Why didn't you put something on?"

"I was in a hurry," she said. Her teeth were chattering. She was trying to cozy up to me and I was trying to escape. Her skin was raw and clammy, like a plucked bird's.

"Any blood this time?"

"I don't think so. I couldn't really see."

"Mm. Still having the pains?"

"Darn right. Unh. Here comes one now, matter of fact. Unh. Oooonh!"

Her initial grunts were tentative. At first she lay rigid, her face without expression except for a kind of thoughtful squint around the eyes. Her breath had caught on the exhale of "oooonh." She was like a huntress surprised into motionlessness by the unexpected appearance of the prey she was stalking. She contemplated it for a bit and then, as the pain welled, she began to work her legs. She flexed her knees, alternately drawing up one and stretching stiff the other. Her mouth widened into a grimace. She arched her back and clenched her fists. "Ooo-oof!" she finally exclaimed. Her whole body shivered in a conclusive convulsion of relief. She breathed deeply and turned her head to smile at me. Features

76

slightly pinched. "Hey," she said, "that was a pretty *good* one!"

"It didn't seem to last too long," I observed. Not because I wasn't empathetic. I was trying to point out the bright side.

"Hn!" she snorted. "Maybe not, but they're getting closer together. And they're getting stronger, too."

"Yeah, but you did okay on that one."

"Mmm...."

"What's the interval now, would you say?"

"I don't know, hard to tell. About ten minutes, I guess."

I found a tiny bump on the inside of my lower lip. I worked it over with my teeth. "Shit. We ought to have a clock. How far apart did that doctor say you should start for the hospital?"

"Why?"

"I was just wondering. When we could consider things were getting serious."

"I'll let you know, Roger. Don't worry."

"Oh, I'm not," I countered. I was miffed by her curtness. I rolled over, turning my back to her. "This sort of stuff could go on for hours anyway," I said. Gloatingly, as a kind of threat. "So I'm going to get my customary beauty rest, and I'd advise you to do the same. Give me a shake when you need me. That is, of course, if you *should* happen to need me."

"It better not," she declared. "I plan to have the shortest, sweetest labor on record."

"Huh? Oh. Okay. Well, good luck.... Relax, then, and get some sleep."

"You know what did this?" she announced suddenly, triumphant with accusal.

"You know what started this? Your screwing me this afternoon! *That's* what did it. I wasn't supposed to go into labor for another two weeks. You're the one who's to blame, I'll have you know. It's your fault. So I'd appreciate a little sympathy."

"Oh. Yeah, right."

"That doctor said I shouldn't have sexual relations for six weeks before delivery."

"Sharon, *hell!*" I yelped, twisting onto my back. "You told me that bastard told you you weren't supposed to fuck for six *months* before delivery! He doesn't *approve* of sexual congress during pregnancy, you said. Remember? In fact I get the idea he doesn't approve of sexual congress at all. Especially among the young and among the *hippies*. Who might, ugh, actually *enjoy* it! Right? And... anyway... you said you weren't going to pay any attention to that, because Anita told you her doctor said there wasn't any reason to have any restrictions at all when she was pregnant. Right?"

"I know."

"And besides, as I recall it was you who made all the overtures this afternoon. You're the one who took off your clothes and flaunted your fantastic naked charms in front of me. All rosy and juicy and big-bellied with child...."

"Big-bellied...."

"About as sexual as it gets. And then when I got a little bit excited, it was you who started urging me to poke my rod up inside there. You remember that? It wasn't my idea. I was perfectly content to just sit there and quietly manipulate myself. If that was your will. Which it wasn't. I was *seduced!*"

"Ha!"

"Ha."

We both lay silent for a while. I chewed the bump.

"You don't really," I finally murmured, "think I had anything to do with it, do you?"

"I do, actually."

"Hm...." I caught a soft strip of lipskin and peeled it away. "Well, maybe so."

"But don't worry, Roger, I don't think there's anything wrong with that. I'm glad we made love. And I'm just as happy to have it get started early, like I said, before. I was just kidding about blaming you. I should be thanking you."

"Yes. You certainly should be."

"And here's a thanks."

She rolled sideways and kissed my mouth. It was a strange sensation, because I was still teasing the tiny piece of skin between my front teeth. For a second I thought of transferring it into her mouth, as a kind of joke. Then I decided she wasn't in the mood for that kind of joking. I swallowed and puckered. Our lips settled together.

"You aren't too upset about what's happening," she asked when the caresses subsided, "are you, Roger... I mean, that it's starting tonight and all?"

"No! Of course not, baby!"

"That's good. Gee, I'm so excited! It's finally going to be over with. *I'm* going to have a *child! Your* child!"

I put my arm around her and pulled her toward me again.

"Uh-oh," she grunted. She edged away and strained through another thirty seconds of pain.

"Yes," I noted to the air, "they seem to be coming like regular clockwork now, all right."

"Listen," Sharon said when she had regained her composure, "you get some sleep, Roger. I'm going to too. We still have lots of time left. Okay?"

"Okay, baby. I'll be right here." I sought her hand and squeezed. "Just give me a prod if you need anything. Even if it's just a little comforting. And remember, relax. Don't get uptight. This is the most natural thing in the whole world. Nothing to get excited about. Happens all the time. Right? Thousands... *hundreds* of thousands of times every day, all over the globe." Squeeze again.

She smiled and nodded.

I'm not sure I could have slept, though, if my head had been perfectly straight. But there was still pot percolating in my brainium to doze me off. Sharon must have been pretty worn out too. Every so often I would kind of surface in response to a groan or a ponderous change of position. But in between, all was quiet. And once I even heard her give off two or three little snores. So we were both apparently knocked out when the dam bust.

Shwhoooosh!

I was lying on my stomach with my left leg slighly drawn up, touching Sharon's. She was sleeping on her back. We like to maintain subliminal physical contact like that. Suddenly I felt her kick, or twitch, or something. A vague accompanying sound splashed in my preconscious.

"Uh!" I heard her exclaim.

Her knee shot up and mine slipped off under it. Right into a sopping splotch of liquid, cooling fast.

"Whuh...?" I grunted.

"Oh Jesus," Sharon breathed, struggling into a sitting position.

"What's up? Is something wrong?"

Her legs, where we touched, were dripping wet. And the mattress under me, as far as I could determine, was soaked.

"What happened?" I persisted. I sat up too, wriggling as best I could out of range of the spreading waters. My heart was drumming a mad mazurka.

Sharon started to chuckle. I rubbed my eyes in the darkness.

"God, look! I'm drenched!" she exclaimed.

I jumped out of bed to make a light. I was scared and confused. The ambient cold immediately attacked me in my areas of dampness. I stumbled and limped around on my slippery bare soles, whimpering as I groped for matches. Finally I got a candle lit. I half-expected to see a wizened baby flopping on the mattress.

"That was really weird!" Sharon declared.

"Jesus fucking Christ!" My blood was sour with adrenalin. "What a way to wake up! What in the hell?"

But by this time, the question was more or less academic.

Sharon laughed. "Beautiful! My bag of waters just broke. That's gotta be it! I was fast asleep and all of a sudden I just felt this big spurt. Look! God! Wow!"

She was sitting at the head of the mattress with her legs akimbo. A trail of yellow-grey water spots led from her vagina to a large oval stain on the mattress cover. Still glistening.

"Huh!" I contributed, peering down at the fluid curiously.

"What a mess! It's all over everything!"

"That's okay," I reassured her. "We'll clean it up."

I stuck the tip of my index finger into the wettest section. Rubbed thumb and finger together, testing for viscosity. Then sniffed. No particular stickiness and no particular aroma. Strange stuff, this amniotic liquor. The waters of life.

According to the book I had just read, the baby—our kid—had been swallowing some and then pissing it right back. There he was, up in there, floating around in his own bodily secretions. Nasty thought. Though not so nasty, I guess, when you stop to consider. I mean I always take a leak when I swim in the ocean. Dogpaddle out a ways, stare nonchalantly at the horizon, open the valve, tread water to stir the effluent in with the other elements, then swim back to the shore—face down, why not? Peculiarly pleased. It's that wombal situation recreated, no doubt.

I wondered if this stuff resembled ocean water. Chemically? Probably not. I read it's a kind of poison. Although so is sea water, if you drink too much of it. Couldn't be too volatile, though, this amniotic fluid. I wondered if it had a taste. If I were to lick it, it would represent some kind of ultimate acceptance of the essences of my woman and my baby, wouldn't it? Hm....

"Roger, would you get me a towel or something?" Sharon requested. "I'm going to catch pneumonia sitting here like this. What a mess!"

"Aren't you interested in...?"

"Yeah, I'm interested. But I'm also soaking wet."

I reached into the pile of dirty clothes in the corner and flipped her one of my old grey tee-shirts. "Here. Use this to dry off with."

She blotted her thighs and calves and scrubbed at the stains. "Damn. How am I going to be able to sleep on this bed now?"

"We'll turn it over."

"Yeah, but.... Unh! Oh darn it.... Uuuuummm...."

Abruptly she stiffened her spine. She cupped her hands, reversed, over her hips and pressed her fingertips hard into the small of her back. Trapping the growing pain in her pelvis as she arched away from it. She craned her head and gritted her teeth, gasping: "Ooof-ooof-ooof! " Her blond hair fell back in ripples to the mattress cover. "Ow-wowtch, Roger! This God damn hurts!"

She lowered herself on her elbows, slowly, creeping sideways until she could extend her legs on a dry section of mattress. "Aaaa-aaargh!" she said. Experimentally. "Aaaiiieeeeee. No. Aaaargh! Is better."

The influence of the comics on our ejaculations is wondrous to contemplate.

I stood idly by, contemplating it irritably for about two seconds. I scowled at my fingers, waiting for the dolor to pass.

When it did I kicked Sharon out of bed and wrestled the mattress around. It thumped over with a cloud of dust. I brushed off as much dirt as I could from the underside.

"You want to put the sheet down now?"

Sharon was standing over by our clothes—I had rigged up a line to hang them from across the opposite corner—fastening the belt of her sweater, which she had just put on. "I guess so," she said.

"The pains are coming pretty fast now... pretty close

together," I observed. "Aren't they?"

"Mm-hm."

"And I guess the bag of waters breaking just about clinches it, eh?" The question was rhetorical. To assure her of that I immediately added: "Because according to what I was just reading, the rupture of the amniotic sac is usually followed within about six hours by labor."

"Golly, that's interesting, Roger. Except I'm already *in* labor, remember? At least I would assume that's what it is. Unless your seafood cookery has given me the worst case of indigestion I ever had!"

"Hm. Yes, um, that's a very good point," I conceded. I curled my lip.

"God, I hope it doesn't go on for another *six hours!*"

"I was thinking in terms of labor meaning delivery," I explained. "You're right. Pardon my confusion. But you know what else I read? The average length of labor for a first birth is about thirteen hours. But the most commonly observed figure for a first baby is seven hours. So...."

"Aren't we the walking compendium of little-known medical facts?" she scoffed.

"Indeed. R. Nall, O.B.-G.Y.N. (Honorary). At your service, madam. Ask me anything. Go ahead. Hit me right here between the eyes. As hard as you can."

"Okay, doctor. What I would like to know is... can I lie down again now?"

"Hmp." I bent back to my bed-making chores. I got out the sheet we'd carefully cleaned and folded away for just this occasion and spread it over the mattress. I smoothed out the wrinkles and tucked the ends and corners under while Sharon paced back and forth, waiting for her next contraction and hoping it would hold off until she was horizontal. She looked funny, with her torso bundled into the bulky knit sweater, her belly bulging out from under the skirts and her lower body naked. It seemed an unfeminine mode of habiliment.

Or dishabiliment. Just the sort of thing that only this most feminine of distractions could promote. While, come to think of it, here I was squatting unmasculinely over a hospital corner.

Birth, the ultimate sexual establisher, was, in a secondary sense, somehow screwing up our roles.

When I was finished Sharon sandwiched herself under the covers. And just in time, because she was immediately hit by another set of pains. While she writhed I put on my clothes. The full array, this time — boots, pants, shirt, sweater. Laying down the sheet had been a benchmark in the delivery process. It was an acknowledgment that our invisible humanoid had, indeed, started clawing his or her way down the cervical tract and could be expected to emerge in the very, very foreseeable future. I would no longer be sharing the bed with Sharon. She and the kid had it all to themselves for their struggle.

HEXAGRAM 5

HSÜ

CALCULATED INACTION

...To accord with the circumstances now prevailing, action must be avoided. Danger lies ahead; but, with firmness and strength, we shall avoid failure....

When she was breathing easy again, I said, "Listen, babe... um... I guess this is kind of the moment of truth."

Sharon propped her pillow against the wall and pushed herself back into a sitting position. She arranged the blankets over her stomach and folded her hands. She looked at me squarely but didn't say anything.

I hunched in front or her. Paused, my forehead wrinkled. "How do you feel?"

"About the way I'd expect I'd feel, Roger. Fine in between the pains, not so hot when they're actually going on. Right at the height, you know... they really do hurt. A lot worse than before. But... it goes away."

"Yeah."

"And comes again."

"Mm-hm."

"And, of course, I suppose things are going to start getting a lot worse from here on in before they get better."

"Yeah, probably. I guess. Maybe."

She shrugged.

"Did it hurt when the bag of waters broke?" I asked. "Were you having a contraction?"

"*No,*" she said. She squirmed and brightened with enthusiasm. "No, that was really the funniest sensation. I mean it wasn't even a sensation at all, really. It was like something happening outside of me. I just suddenly woke up when I felt this big sploosh between my legs." She laughed. "For a second I thought maybe I'd lost control of my bladder. That's kind of what it felt like, I guess. A huge involuntary piss. Only different. There was no relief or anything. Not really much feeling at all, except getting wet. And certainly no pain."

"Good."

We both fell silent. Sharon's face grew more somber.

"So...," I said. "Well.... So what do you think?"

She stared at me unhelpfully.

"Hmmm?" I persisted.

"About what?"

"You know." I locked in on her pupils. "Do you want to go to the hospital?"

She returned my stare thoughtfully. Chin tipped up, betraying no response.

"I mean... if we leave now we can probably get there in plenty of time. Right? Time to spare. But if we wait too much longer it'll be too late. To change our minds. Probably. You know, unless something.... Well...."

"Why, Roger? Do you want me to?"

"*No,* baby! No. It doesn't make any difference to me, one way or the other. I mean... what I really mean is, it should be your decision completely. Hell, I can't know how you're feeling."

"True."

"Yeah, true. So it's got to be up to you. You already know perfectly well all my ideas on the subject."

"I guess. Unless you're starting to change your mind. Maybe you're getting worried now."

"*No!* Believe me, not the least bit. It's just that... well, figure. This is hardly the sort of thing a person can make up his... excuse me, make up *her* mind about absolutely and irrevocably just completely in the abstract. Right? I mean sure, it's all very fine and well and good, you know, to say with big bluff bravado that you're going to just have your baby at home... six months before it happens. To say that then. Piff, tut." I snapped my fingers. "But the point is, how do you feel about it when you're actually cramping and moaning and bleeding and it comes right down to the gritty-nitty? How *do* you feel about it? Maybe you'd like to have a nice, sympathetic, qualified doctor hovering over you, and a lot of fluttering nurses in starched white uniforms and stuff. Anesthetics and sterile dressings and a chrome-plated delivery room. Get wheeled in under the flourescent lights and get your cunt shaved and get strapped onto the table like a prisoner in the electric chair. And then get a big whiff of gas and you're knocked out cold, and out pops Plastic Baby and you never knew what hit you. Maybe that's more your style. I mean maybe the pain is getting to be stiffer than you can bear, or you're afraid or something. I don't know."

"Gee, you certainly do paint an inviting picture."

"I do?"

"Lovely. It's so unbiased."

I grinned.

"No, Roger, I agree with you. I always have. The only possible thing I've ever had in mind about it is whether it's dangerous for the baby."

"Yeah. Well, sure.... I suppose under some circumstances it could be. There's danger in everything."

"I think the pain, you know, I can take."

"Women have been for centuries!"

She nodded.

"And as far as danger is concerned.... Okay, first of all, if something starts to go wrong we can jump right in the car and head for the hospital...."

"I can see that. Me with the baby stuck half in and half out, dashing for the car...."

I batted the objection away with both hands. "Don't worry! Believe me, I'd trundle you outside and into that back seat in about fourteen seconds. No sweat. Necessity of the mother speeds invention."

"Hn!"

"And as far as the second thing, there's higher infant mortality in hospitals than anyplace else."

She hoisted an ironic eyebrow. "Right. Could that be,

91

you know, because more infants are born in hospitals these days?"

"Well.... No. No, I don't think so. The rate's higher. At least I believe that's the case. Because of all the germs. You know, hospitals are supposed to be so sterile, but they're actually the place where all our society's disease germs are concentrated."

"Whatever."

"Around here all we've got is regular house bugs. Cholera, plague, hepatitis...."

She ignored the leaden levity. "It would still take an awfully long time to get there," she said. "As you just said yourself, a minute ago."

"Forty minutes." Maybe if we averaged eighty, I admitted to myself. "Hour. Max. Probably less. If we're careful we shouldn't have any emergency that would happen too fast for that to be enough, though. Should we?"

My knees had begun to register a complaint at my hunker. I stood up stiffly. "But we've been all over this before. Sure there's risk. There's risk in getting pregnant. Everything in life is bound up in risk. And death."

I took a few aimless steps, walking out the stiffness. I was a little sorry I had mentioned death. "Darn it all, baby...." I scuffed my toe along the edge of a warped floorboard. "Don't *listen* to me! It's easy enough for me to talk. I'm not lying there, experiencing what you're experiencing. That's the whole point of this. I'm not trying to be callous. I'm not some Svengali, trying to talk you into doing something that goes against your natural grain... your better judgment. Just because I've got a bunch of crackpot ideas about natural functions. I don't want to endanger your health or the baby's. That's the last thing I want to do. But maybe I am. Maybe I'm a complete nut. Which is why I'm having second thoughts. Now's the time to have them, not a couple of hours from now when it's too late. Right? So what do you think? You're the one who's got to decide."

"Roger, I already made up my mind a long time ago. I don't see any reason to change it now."

"You're sure?"

"Yeah. Having a kid is child's play."

"I don't think that's quite the right metaphor...."

"Shut up and give me a kiss."

"You're sure this isn't going to get more painful later on?" I asked.

"No, I'm *not* sure. In fact I'm sure it *is!* But I think I can stand it. As long as you're here. Now come down beside me and give me a kiss." She patted the mattress imperiously.

"And you're not scared stiff by the prospect of my amateur midwifery?"

"A little wobbly, maybe, but not stiff."

"Let's see... where did I put the pliers?"

"Ha ha, very amusing. Kiss, doctor!"

I stooped in compliance. But just as I nestled alongside her, I felt her body vibrate with an odd resonance.

"See, darn it?" she wailed. "You waited too long!"

She drew back and braced herself to absorb the throes. There wasn't much I could do. I stroked her thigh and murmured soothing encouragements. At least I hoped they were soothing. Sharon was a little too busy and introverted to let me know one way or the other. Until it was over, that is. Then she grabbed my hand and gave me a kind of fuzzy, hungry, damp-eyed look and all of a sudden lunged sideways and practically melted against me.

"Oh Roger," she breathed. Into my mouth. Her tongue curled passionately over mine. And this was followed by a sigh so hot and deep I was surprised my vocal cords didn't hum in response. To be frank, that kind of kiss is something of a rarity after two years together. It should be savored—and returned in kind, vertiginously. But darned if I wasn't so uptight now about all the things I was going to have to do in order to get ready to deliver Sharon of child that I couldn't muster the proper mindless emotion. So I gave her the best I could—some play-acting, temporizing kisses—and happily accepted the love or gratitude or whatever it was she felt impelled to bestow. And I'm sure my mummery was less than deceptive.

"I love you, baby," I said finally, trying to compensate with words. I cupped the back of her head in my hand. Lush plaits of hair streamed between my fingers. I fondled the nape of her neck, so soft and vulnerable... and the swell of her skull, eggshell fragile, erogenous. "Man, do I ever!"

"You'll take care of me, won't you?"

"Oh *Christ!*" I pressed her to me. Roughly, almost involuntarily. Her ardor, and the realization that she was surrendering herself—her diploid self—completely into my hands, actually made me queasy. My stomach tightened and my ribcage clenched. "Yes, Sharon," I said. "I will. Jesus, yes!'

"We'll have a beautiful baby. Right here in the middle of the forest. With nobody to interfere."

"Right. The way it's been done for a billion years."

"And you'll be my doctor."

"Doctor Feelgood."

"And everything will go swimmingly. And I'll put him right to my breast."

"Mm. Him?"

She leaned away and smiled up into my face. "Yeah."

I grinned dubiously. "Okay. Okay by me."

"It'll all be fantastic."

"Absolutely."

"I love you, Roger."

But suddenly I was worried again. I had allowed us to get carried away. In my teleology there is a Fate — arbitrary, of course, but prone to malevolence — whom one must not tempt by the folly of expressing expectations (except, maybe, in order to wring some bitter satisfaction out of a last laugh, the worst).

That was why, for example, I had put off any premature

consideration of Sharon's *accouchement*. There was always the possibility of miscarriage. If you live for the moment alone, I maintain, Fate is fucked. It can only get you when your guard is down — when you're gazing idyllically toward a cloudless horizon. Sure as shit there'll be a typhoon boiling beneath the curve. Or you'll get hit on the head by a meteorite.

So you've got to dig actuality and not get hung up on potentiality. As long as you stay scrupulously locked into now — and bear in mind the ultimate certainty, Death — the good is ecstatic and the bad is no worse than neutral. At least that's the way I figure it. Maybe it's a kind of kinky hubris. Psychic one-upmanship. An unwillingness to admit that anything can hurt. I know nature's got me by the balls: The object is never to give it satisfaction by forgetting.

Howsomeever....

I had better, I thought nervously, create a diversion. I rapped on the wall behind me with my knuckles and cleared my throat.

"All right," I said. "Well now, be that as it may, I think it's time for me to get busy."

I squeezed her arm, smiled assuringly and hauled myself to my feet.

HEXAGRAM 6

SUNG

CONFLICT

...In this hexagram, the upper trigram indicates firmness; the lower, danger. When danger is met by firmness, conflict follows.... It would be unwise to cross the great river (go on any journey) as we should inevitably tumble into the watery abyss....

The first thing I did was to assemble all our candles and deploy them in various strategic locations around the room. I lighted two more, but saved the rest to make sure there'd be a reserve. Under the best of circumstances this was not exactly going to be a brilliantly illuminated operation. Then I started calculating. The time now, I figured, must be about one or two a.m. I supposed Sharon's contractions were coming at pretty close to five-minute intervals. So, although you couldn't be precise about these things, it seemed likely she'd give birth before daylight. If everything kept on at its present pace. I chuckled to myself. The kid was going to have the perfect background to run for president. A frontier heritage: "My parents homesteaded the frontiers of consciousness. Headed west in flight from technology." Or something like that.

The next consideration was heat. The room was too cold. Sharon was going to have to be uncovered during the final stages—and anyway, newborn babies are supposed to be kept warm. We didn't really have any source of heat except the kitchen stove. So I went outside and chopped up a bunch of kindling.

The moon had set, and my first footfall was greeted by scampering paws somewhere off behind the shed. My eyes hadn't yet adjusted to the dark. Raccoons I guessed. They'd probably duck into the bushes and watch me warily from behind their masks until the coast was clear. Then resume breaking and entering.

I grabbed my axe and went around back, where bunches of fallen boughs were stacked against the wall. I reached into the tangle and dragged out my first victim. It scratched and struggled all the way. I dismembered it skillfully, and then hewed the body into six stove-sized pieces. When I had amassed an armful, I carried the faggot inside. I dumped it into the orange crate by the stove. I was examining my bare forearms for blood or scars—the kind that hinted of permanence—when a small rubbercolored spider peeked out from under my rolled-up right sleeve. It dashed south, but prudently—just before my swatting hand swashed down—parachuted after the kindling. I let it float to earth and scuttle to safety among the sticks before I separated its silken shroud from my brachioradial. Then I stoked up the stove. When I had a goodly flame chuffing in the innards, I opened the oven door and uncovered all the burners. Pretty soon waves of warmth were shimmering across the kitchen. Before long, I hoped, they would wash into the other room.

Meanwhile, Sharon was doing her thing.

"How's it going, baby?" I inquired brightly, leaning around the doorway.

She had sagged lower, and now lay drowsily with only her head bolstered. "Mm," she said, starting to make a face and then abandoning the effort. "Okay, I guess."

"Do you need me there?"

She stuck out her lower lip to emphasize, and belie, her stoicism. "Nope."

"Sure?"

She nodded sadly.

"Because I got the fire going.... Does it feel any warmer?"

"A little."

"Okay, just hang on a bit. Do they hurt a lot?"

"Yeah."

I frowned. "I bet." I walked into the room and went and crouched beside her. I picked up her hand and kneaded it with my thumb and then ran the knuckle of my other hand down the side of her cheek. Embarrassingly false and futile comforts. "I'm sorry, baby," I commiserated. "I wish I could share it with you."

Like shit. No sense in compounding the hypocrisy. "As a matter of fact," I admitted, "I really don't. But...." I rubbed her hand some more. "You're going to be a little soldier, aren't you?"

"Fuck no!" The sally amused her.

"Still full of pepper. Good sign. You're doing okay."

She smiled grimly.

I jumped up. So much to do, so much to do. Let's see....

I went into the kitchen to get a pile of newspapers— I'm not sure for exactly what purpose. Soak up blood, I guess. Anyway you never know when newspapers'll come in handy in a situation like this. As I brought the sheaf back to Sharon's room I noticed that the topmost page—the cover from a yellowed *Barb*—bore a full-length photograph of a naked chick. Shaggy pussy the focal point, given its rarity in journalism, of the composition. My first reaction was physical. A kind of muffled inguinal ignition. I scanned the lubricious grey image feeling the way a gas heater sounds when its burners are touched off by the pilot light. Then I had my second reaction, and it instantly snuffed out the first. I wondered if Sharon had cleansed her vagina and environs.

"Hey," I proposed, dropping the papers, "we've got to wash you off, you know."

"Huh? Mm."

"Lots of hot water, that's what we need. Soap and water. Get you squeaky clean down there."

"Yik."

"Figure of speech."

I hurried out to the pump with a big stewpot. Once again my emergence from the cabin set up animal commotions in the darkness. I primed the pump and filled the pot with frigid well water. When it splashed against my fingers it bit like acid. I lugged the pot inside, holding it awkwardly out in front of me so the contents wouldn't slosh on my bell-bottoms. I set it on the stove to simmer. By now the kitchen was warm enough for shirtsleeves, and a tepid sector had radiated through the door to the foot of Sharon's mattress.

In the corner under her hanging clothes stood a pair of cardboard boxes, lashed sloppily with twine. They held the assortment of infant paraphernalia we had managed to scrounge from friends. Or rather, Sharon had. I wasn't certain what was in them. This seemed like the time to find out. I dragged the boxes into the center of the floor and fought a brief match with the knots. My fingers lost, of course. I retired to the kitchen for a knife, ruefully rubbing the bloodless blue furrows the twine had gouged across my palm.

When I opened the first box I found it contained diapers. Stacks of them—soft, slightly frayed rectangles of off-white cotton, stitched double-thickness down the middle for absorbency. There must have been more than a hundred. What in the hell, I wondered, did we need so many for? But then I reflected: A baby must piss... how much, maybe fifty times a day? And need a change at least a dozen? I had a sudden, sodden picture of those diapers, all crumpled and yellow and soggy, emanating palpable ripples of uric reek. This was immediately expanded into the even more disquieting realization—my coprophilic mind's eye once again supplying vivid imagery—that in three out of every ten cases the folds would reveal a central blob of slimy green baby ordure. Yuuuch. Thank God Sharon was going to be in charge of sanitary engineering.

But this gave rise to still another concern: How were we going to wash these things? Had anybody devoted any thought to that? Somehow I doubted that Sharon was going to last long crooked over a washboard and galvanized tub every couple of days. Scouring the shit out of kiddy's fertile breechclouts. And I couldn't see me chugging off to the local laundromat three times a week—coughing and gasping through the fumes for forty miles. Well, maybe I was being too pessimistic. What do they do about diapers in jungle villages? Get along without 'em, probably. Let Baby do business in the dust. At any rate, we could be thankful we had diapers enough to postpone that crisis for a while.

I sawed through the twine cinching the second box. This one contained a more varied collection of goodies. First there were some thin cotton blankets which I took out and set aside. Azure teddy bears rampant on a field of alphabet blocks gules. Then there was a pile of linen which, upon unfolding, turned out to be crib sheets. Nice for whenever we got a crib. Then there were a couple of heavy felt mats with serrated edges—something to protect the crib's mattress against baby's overflows, I guessed. Then there were three pairs of plastic panties. The elastic was sprung around the waist of one and the leg of another. But equine benefactions ought not be scrutinized for dental caries.

I seemed to be getting groggy.

Well! I came upon a card bearing four outsize safety pins. I tossed those over on top of the diapers. And next a bunch of clothes: little white cotton anklets and tee-shirt tops and pastel sleeper suits with drop-seats. I held one up. It was light green terry-cloth, embroidered on the breast with a white puppy. There were tassels on the toes. I used the embroidery and tassels to orient myself—legs and arms all looked the same. What impressed me was the size.

"Medium," the label said, "Birth To 20 Pounds."

Until then I had not really stopped to think how big a newborn baby would be. How small, I ought to say. If this minuscule sheath represented twenty pounds of infant—I tried to visualize a protruding head and hands—then what would a newly-hatched eight-pounder look like?

Phew. According to the book, as I recalled, the average baby comes out about twenty inches long. I tried to judge twenty inches with my hands. The way you describe a fish. Come to think of it, that was a pretty good basis for comparison. A newborn baby would be about the size of a trout. Only lumpier. And less efficiently designed. Amazing. Especially if you consider that Sharon has to squeeze it out through her vagina. Brrr. My testicles hopped up in horror at the thought. I wadded the suit into a ball and stuffed it back in the box. I rooted to the bottom. There were two plastic rattles, one shaped like a dogbone, the other wearing a once-smiling cartoon mouse-face. The features had been gummed into semi-eclipse by the previous owner. But it still rattled quite adequately. I slid that box into the corner, piled the blankets in with the diapers and shoved the diaper-box off to one side—but easily accessible—with my foot. Over my shoulder I could see steam lowering in the kitchen. The water must be boiling.

I had to go out and get some cold water to dilute what was on the stove. When I came back I heard Sharon moaning. I left the bucket on the kitchen floor and rushed in to make sure nothing unusual was happening. I found her going through her supine walking-in-place motions under the blanket. But the contractions were waning. She took a few deep breaths to relax. I told her I was going to wash her.

"Okay," she said, "but first let me go to the bathroom."

I helped her to her feet and made her put on her sandals. I didn't think she ought to be trekking out to the shithouse alone in the dark, but she insisted. She preceded me through the kitchen door, taking very careful steady steps—and looking around at me to make sure I was noticing. I sure as hell was.

"Hey, watch...!"

Too late, of course. Her right root struck the bucket, toppled it sideways and came down on the lip. A freezing cataract sluiced over her ankles. She shrieked and hobbled for balance. The leather sandal-soles skidded out from under her. Her right hand described a tiny, futile circle—not so much a grab for equilibrium as a poignant farewell wave. She heeled gracefully, but disastrously, to the left. Past her righting moment. For an eyeblink she seemed to hang there, at a forty-five-degree angle, proudly unbent, like some noble collapsing building. The Empire State, perhaps, with King Kong clinging to the fifty-second floor. And just as gravity gave the triumphant jerk... my wrist snaked under her armpit.

Whump. One hundred and forty-five pounds of kinetic energy played concerti on my ligaments. My knees buckled. Sharon struck the floor with the point of her ass-bone, splatted awkwardly in the pool of water. But survived. I had broken her fall.

I spent the next minute or two running articulation tests on my arm.

And embroidering the kitchen air with scato-theological commentary. Sharon sat at my shins, whimpering. She had scared herself. But where she would normally have remained inert for a long time, letting the shock wear off, tonight her cold-water cushion spurred quick recovery. She lumbered to her feet with a grudging assist from my good hand. Apparently it was in her interest not to be injured. Once I had satisfied myself of that, I worked out my own fright in another spate of profanity.

Sharon swabbed herself off with a dishtowel, avoiding my eyes.

"I'm sorry, Roger," she finally mumbled. "Is your arm all right?"

"Is *my arm* all right? Fucking shit! Is *your body* all right?"

She hung the towel over the edge of the table, looking at me. "Yeah," she nodded.

I rubbed my aching shoulder.

She went outside. I snatched up the bucket and followed

her. Her back was fading toward the outhouse. I started to yell something like, "So what if I can never give my Carnegie Hall recital now!"—some twinkling, ostensibly benign comment that would lead us into the customary argument. But I caught myself. The pattern was this: Since she was not hurt, I felt entitled to be. And that would require bullying. Because she would defend her clumsiness by attacking me for leaving the bucket in her path. And I would smother my guilt in an explosion of blame for not watching where she was going. And she would say that she could have been killed—with trumps, the unborn baby. And I would exact my thanks for saving her lives by playing up my own injury. And she would express her gratitude by finally accepting this inverted outlay of sympathy. Except....

Except she wasn't following the script. Which meant she really was hurt. Or told me more about the state of her labor than any moaning or groaning could.

I peeled off toward the pump and drew water. I kept a sentinel eye on the dim smudge made by the outhouse against the trees. When I realized I could make out the cracks between the individual boards, I began to worry. She was taking an awfully long time. I considered going down to find out if anything was the matter. Then I decided I was being too edgy. At the same time it occurred to me that I had earned some recompense for my evening's troubles. And fortification against those to come. A beer sure would go good. I went over to the house and reached behind the rear corner cinder block and fished a can out of the cooler-tub. Hooo-*whee!* *¡Ay! ¡Chihuahua!* I shook the icy water from my fingertips and hastily dried the hand on my pants between the knees. I popped the top and took a swig. Sharon still hadn't come out. I went back and stood by the bucket. Drank another swallow. Changed hands because the wet aluminum numbed. Started strolling toward the outhouse, warming my free paw under my armpit. I snapped a twig as I neared the door.

"That you, Roger?"

I froze and didn't say anything for a minute. Then I began to growl. Low and menacing—and building up to my most violent imitation of an ursine roar. At the climax my voice betrayed me with a squeak. I cleared my throat.

"Smoky the Bear," I announced gruffly. "Crush out all smokes. And spread your legs."

"You scared me."

"Everything," I asked jauntily, "coming out all right?"

There was no immediate response from the interior. I listened for movements, squirts, panting—clues to what might be going on. I heard none.

"Funny you should ask," she said finally. Her voice sounded weak, but maybe it was just the intervening door. "I think that's exactly what's happening."

"What?"

More silence. Then....

"Well, not quite yet. Pretty soon, though."

"What? What do you mean? What's the trouble?"

The door swung open. I stepped back and Sharon appeared. She was moving deliberately and holding on to the jamb.

"Are you okay?" I blurted.

"Yeah, yeah."

I went up and took her arm. She didn't put any weight on me, but I could feel her poised to lean if she should have to.

"Did you hurt yourself when you fell?"

"No, unh-unh, Roger. No, I'm sure that hasn't got anything to do with it. Well...."

"It probably didn't help any either, though."

"I was just going to say that. I had another contraction in there."

We walked back toward the house. I veered and picked up the bucket. Sharon waited until I was beside her again, then grasped the inside of my arm. We proceeded very slowly, in step. She seemed kind of wobbly now. With that special Newtonian sense that adjacent masses have of each other, I could detect her center or gravity—considerably lower than before. We were nearing the cabin when she halted me.

"Wait a second," she said.

I stopped. I looked down at her. Her bottom lip was sucked in, gripped tightly by her front teeth. Her free hand was resting on the underswell of her stomach. The hand clutching my arm was tense—and clenching tighter, the fingers digging in around my tendons. In fact, it was starting to hurt, but I didn't say anything. I leaned sideways and set the bucket on the ground. I took the can of beer out of my encumbered fist.

"Just relax, Sharon," I said. "Don't fight it."

"Oh, brother," she grunted.

"Easy. Let it come."

"Yeh. Yeh. Unh! You... try... unh... try it sometime."

"Just hang on."

That was a pretty unnecessary piece of advice. Sharon was clamped to the crook of my arm like a pentopus.

"Oh... Jesus... Christ!" She was beginning to fold up around her pain. First at the waist—or rather the hips, since she had no waist—and then at the knees. Stiffly, cumbersomely, she sank to her haunches. But she kept her spine straight and her head far back. As she squatted there like that she reminded me of a Russian dancer. It was probably something akin to hysteria on my part—because a picture of her suddenly breaking into Cossack kicks flitted across my mind. I almost laughed out loud—a laugh I know would have rung with brittle panic. I swallowed and looked into her eyes. They were fixed on me, but no sight was coming out. Her mouth was contorted, the corners drawn wide. Her teeth were set and a nerve jittered at the base of her jaw. The hair framing her face clung to the skin greasily.

"Take deep breaths," I said. "Try not to let your muscles

110

tense."

She nodded distractedly at my cool reason. Then cried out, sobbing, shouting in real anguish: "Uuunh! Oh, Roger! Oh.... *oooonh!*"

I was rubbing the meat of my palm across her talon fingers. Trying to knead in solicitude. I still held the beer can. "It's okay. It's okay," I said. "It's okay, baby. It's almost over now."

I found myself straining to lift her. I was afraid the baby would pop out right there on the ground if she maintained that eliminatory position much longer.

Perhaps Sharon had the same idea. Her face was still screwed up against the pain, but she began to haul herself erect. Very, very gradually, like someone on an escalator. A low, constricted moan whistling out with the effort. I could see the muscles in her thighs tremble. And then I noticed, curving into the shadow between her legs, a jagged trickle of blood. My stomach did a flip. There were two dark, damp, ragged spots about the size of quarters in the dust between her sandals.

"Oh Jesus," I exhaled.

Sharon stood upright now. She leaned heavily against me, both hands wrapped around my elbow for support, her face buried in the shoulder of my sweater. Her breath came out in rapid gusts. My heart picked up the same beat—double-time. I squinted at the irregular part gouged across the crown of her hair. Like the meandering blood-trail I had just seen.

"Can you walk now, baby? You think?" My urgency was messing up my vowels.

Sharon's head bobbed. Twitched, more like.

I took a hesitant step toward the house. Sharon shuffled with me. After another couple of hobbles she lifted her head and watched where she was going. Her syncopated respiration was becoming rhythmic again. She sighed and tossed the hair out of her eyes. I felt better now too, concentrating on our progress. *As* we mounted the stairs, like a pair of arthritic old ladies, I saw her cheek in profile. A drying tear-streak glinted in the kitchen light.

We tracked across the wet floor and into the bedroom. I got Sharon down on the mattress but made her lie diagonally, with her feet out. The room was plenty warm. Sharon arranged herself for comfort and smiled at me. She brushed her hair back with her middle fingers. She blinked, wiped the corners of her eyes, finished with a downward swipe to blot her cheeks.

"I guess I'm not being such a soldier," she apologized.

"You're doing fine," I said.

I pulled off her muddy sandals. The balls and heels of her feet were filthy, and dust had caked between her toes. The inside of her left thigh was smeared with a thin, pinkish serum. I had kept the sheet from getting muddy but not, I noticed, from absorbing its first bloody stain. We'd set aside two clean bath towels, like the sheet, especially for the coming event. I wadded up one, stuffed it between her legs. She arched her back so I could push a flattened end under her buttocks.

I stood, sipped some beer, and went to fetch the bucket.

HEXAGRAM 7

SHIH

THE ARMY

*...Persistence in a righteous course
brings to those in authority good
fortune and freedom from error.
If the enquiry is not concerned with
military affairs, we must interpret this
hexagram symbolically in the sense
that life is a battle....*

When Sharon was thoroughly clean from the waist down—
and dry and once more settled under the blankets—I
brought in a chair from the kitchen so I could keep vigil
beside her.

She had had another pain. They were coming only a few
minutes apart now. It was getting harder and harder for me to
ignore them. Sharon was obviously being worn down by this
continual, accelerating internal rack. Though no more, I told
myself, than could or should be expected. That bony bottleneck
I could sometimes feel when I fucked her had to yawn four
inches before the baby could slither through. Only the baby
didn't want to. So the muscular uterine bulb behind it had
started pulsating. Mother Nature's Handy-Dandy Parturitional
Pile-Driver. That's using your head, junior. What had the book
said? Thirty or forty pounds of pressure ramming baby into
the gap.

Ready, kid? Squunch, whump, ooooph! Cervix gives
another millimeter. No wonder an infant's skull is so squishy.
Meet my son, the rivet. Or daughter, as the case may be. Six
or seven hours of that at regular intervals is bound to get on
a woman's nerves.

I tilted my chair back against the wall, hooked my
boot-heels over the rung and rolled a cigarette.

The tobacco pouch, with its drawstring neck, made
the perfect uterine metaphor, I decided.

I drank my beer and wolfed in nicotine. The cigarette,
for some reason, set off echoes of the pot I had smoked earlier.
A sort of lightheadedness, and a photosensitivity that seemed
to extend even to the cells of my skin and hair. The room's

languid heat and lambent shadowlight engulfed me. I felt suspended, like a specimen in a jar. It was very relaxing.

I took a pull on the beercan. I swished the tart liquid around in my mouth. My teeth were fuzzy from lack of brushing, but I could feel the piquant fizz of fermented grain dissolving their coat. I savored the nip of the hops until the chill wore off, then let tiny driblets seep down my throat. My body felt hollow, as though filling from the toes up with the warm alcohol. It was at mid-chest level now and rising rapidly. Both the inside liquid and the outside air were in tepid equilibrium. By a process of osmosis. My skin was a permeable membrane—a loose bag of flesh dangling unaccountably over the solid knob of my skull. It enclosed no recognizably personal substance. Just the percolating alcohol and a rackety jumble of odd floating bones and organs. And in fact, if I were to duck my head too abruptly, the whole outfit might shift. An arm suddenly projecting where the left ear had been. The ear now sprouting like a fungus, a mushroom, from the sagittal suture. The other decorating the neck. Right shoulder down around the waist. Opposite the waggling legs. Weird. Maybe it was the beer as well as the grass. Maybe it was fatigue. Whatever, I let it carry me away.

Until Sharon had another contraction.

I'd long since come to the conclusion that the pangs of birth, as depicted on the silver screen, are greatly exaggerated. And until recently, the silver screen had provided my only access to the secrets of the delivery room. Except for, oh yeah, a few novels—*A Farewell To Arms, War & Peace*—in which the heroine is more likely than not to expire from the ordeal. Hips too narrow or forceps too brutal or some such routine complication. I remember throughout my adolescence hunching disconsolately into the plush and gritting my popcorn-encrusted molars as the leading lady up there in front of me began to claw at her pillow-padded midriff. Ripping off Academy-Award-decibel screams as she started her gurney journey to the ether machine.

It was bad enough if she were legally wed. But if the *accouchement* were the fruit of fornication, the suffering and its screen time would be trebled or quadrupled. Matter of fact, it occurred to me, the Swedes still go in for that sort of thing. Their sexual mores are supposed to be so free, but the payoff—at least in the cinema—is still straight from some dour Lutheran catechism. Agony lingered upon with prurient intensity. I wondered why Ingmar and Mai failed to transcend that particular hang-up? Anyway, dutiful communicant that I was in my adolescence, I still couldn't figure out why God had supposedly designed the elemental experience to be such torture. Hold down the population? It's true that the people-boom roughly coincides with the introduction of anesthetics. But dogs and cats produce litter after litter without benefit of painkillers. And women go on year after year having babies in the "backward" countries. You'd think they'd have learned, after all these centuries, to stop with one—or at least just a couple. Because if the function of sex is purely reproductive and not to give pleasure—as my priest instructors were then assuring me—there is no adequately balancing rationale to explain the torment of birth. It's just another dirty trick dreamed up by a cruel God. Further harassment of His hapless creations.

Nor is the Puritan ethic much better—although I suppose it is slightly more charitable to the Deity. At least it allows that sex can be fun. If you don't watch. But Puritans make man pay for every drop of pleasure. (Or more accurately, in this case, woman. A curious divine breach of the Civil Rights Act.) Anything that feels as good as a good screw has to have an obverse. Just as any medicine that really works is bound to have an awful taste. Cod-liver oil, piano lessons and frequent spankings to make up for the child labor laws. Nine months of nausea, thirteen hours of excruciation and twenty-one years of responsibility to make up for the clitoris.

119

I think that partly explains the Scandinavians. But then, they may have something else in mind entirely. Perhaps they are saying that sex without joy reaps a joyless reward. Look at all those empty characters fumbling after sensation in a round of random fucking. Who could be more torpid than a Bergman Swede? Embalmed in his bleak, wintry, boiled-potato urban technocracy. Even an Antonioni Italian has some residual oregano spicing his Mediterranean blood. But when one of those *Svenska flickar* flops wearily into the hay, you can be sure she ain't gonna be turning no nip-ups two-hundred-and-eighty days later.

At least that accorded partially with my own theory: that the severity of birth pain is a function of the mind. Still, I dislike seeing birth used as a facile cinematic penance. And I suspect the Swedes are hypocritical besides. All that titty-titty bang-bang may be futile and decadent in the script—but it gives you a proper hard-on.

Anyway, the result of my pimply philosophizing on the subject of birth was a firm conviction that Hollywood's depictions were nothing but propaganda. Nineteenth Century Moralism in Twentieth Century Fox clothing. Imbuing whole generations of possible future lays with a pathological dread of the very process which defines them as women. Womb-men. With, of course, the rest of the attendant sexual screwups. And so I adopted the opposite view. Grounded in total ignorance and wishful theorizing, I decided that childbirth didn't really hurt very much at all. Or, if there were some unusual pain, it could surely be no worse than what I had myself experienced of it. About like mashing your finger in a car door, or having a tooth drilled without novocaine, or breaking your nose on a low tackle, or getting four cold-turkey lip stitches after an ice-hockey game. Unpleasant, sure. But nothing to shriek about.

Only now I was watching Sharon and I was beginning to suspect that my ideas might merit some adjustment.

At least the contractions were intermittent.

When the latest had ceased I sat forward, polished off my beer and deposited the empty can in the kitchen. I had made up my mind that from now on I was going to do more. More than just stand around idly wringing mind and hands. I was going to try to give her immediate physical, as well as moral, encouragement. But in the meantime I thought I had better take advantage of this lull to complete my obstetrical preparations.

The fire in the stove was dying, so I shoved in a new load of kindling. The cabin was really very warm now. I was flushed and sweating after stirring up the flames. I stripped off my sweater. The water in the stewpot had just about boiled away, so I replenished it from the bucket. I thought about the movie cliché: sending the distraught father out to the kitchen to boil water.

"What do you need all that water for, doc?"

"Confidentially, Miz Crenshaw... forceps... I don't. But it gives him something to do."

However, I did need the water—to sterilize our carving knife. I put the knife in the pot, blade-first. Then it occurred to me that I was also going to need something to tie off the umbilical cord once it was cut. I pondered for a moment. Paper clip? Clothes pin? String? I was a little afraid of metals, both because they might scratch the tender baby skin and because they could conceivably be poisonous.

I picked up the childbirth manual from the table and thumbed through it. From my earlier reading I knew just about which page I wanted. Leafing past diagrams of various fetal positions. Breech presentation. Shoulder presentation—one imploring arm reaching out into the birth canal. Brrr. It was that sort of thing that made me shudder. I tapped the tabletop. Let me see the tip of a head, Whatever's In Charge Out There.

I riffled through a couple more pages. Subhead:

121

"Delivery." My scanning eyes stumbled:

"...Early stages, the fetal heart rate and regularity are checked at frequent intervals...."

Nothing about what happens if they're not. Or if the checks reveal inconsistencies. Only implication. Hell, the stethoscope's a relatively recent invention. Maybe a keen ear's enough. The Blackfeet and the Crows didn't have stethoscopes. Scan on:

"...Progress of labor is determined by vaginal examination...."

Shouldn't be too difficult. Just don't poke around with excessive vigor. I wondered if I could gauge ten centimeters. "Sawn-timeters," the nurses always say. Or, for that matter, five. Five sawntimeters. Why don't they just say inches?

Have to start soon, I realized, so I could sense the change, at least. Scan on:

"...Baby's head at floor of vagina... pressure causes the woman to bear down reflexively... anesthesia... performs the episiotomy by incising the perineum with surgical scissors. The operation prevents jagged tears or excessive distension as the emerging head stretches the tissue between the anus and the fourchette of the vulva...."

Hm. Come to think of it, I wondered if I should boil a pair of scissors?

Brrr. Hell no. Nowhere in the Bible does it mention episiotomy. I'm pretty sure. Have to keep this as simple as possible. I'm no surgeon. If it tears, it tears.

Easy for me to say. Shit. Scan on:

"...Head may be eased out by gentle upward pressure on the chin. As it emerges, it will twist spontaneously in the direction of the axis of the shoulders, which are tightly hunched and rotated in the birth canal. The obstetrician, after assuring that the umbilical...."

Ah, *here* we are. I slowed, read more carefully:

"...Cord is not dangerously coiled about the neck or

shoulders, cradles the head in both hands, one under each side of the jaw, and guides the body downward. This permits the uppermost, leading shoulder to slide free. Traction upward will then bring forth the trailing shoulder. Torso and limbs, the diameters of which are considerably less than that of the head, will follow easily...."

Wow. I really ought to commit that to memory, I recognized. It sounded awfully complex—and important. I bent the corner of the page as a marker. I was going to keep the book open here and beside me throughout. However, I still hadn't found what I was originally looking for. Scan on:

"...Child is immediately held upside down by its heels. To insure clear air passages, the mouth and nose are suctioned by aspirator, tube or rubber bulb...."

Good thing I *had* kept on reading. I'd forgotten about that.

"...Crying lustily... breathing regularly... healthy pink color...."

Ah, finally:

"...A clamp resembling a bobby pin is applied to the umbilical cord three inches from the abdomen. The cord is then cut. The stump will dry and fall off within a few days...."

So. A quick check of the rest of the page to make sure there were no other critical references. Not much help, that, really: "a clamp resembling a bobby pin." Well, it was an idea. I guessed Sharon had some of those somewhere floating around. But the clasp of a bobby pin seemed to me kind of loose. I liked my paper clip comparison better. Anyway, I knew for sure where there were a couple of those. And maybe a little string for good measure. Or better yet, thread. Back-up equipment.

I went into the other room and removed two paper clips from rejected manuscripts. Sharon's eyes were closed, and adenoidal snores were issuing from her open mouth. I searched her packing-crate dresser and found a spool of

Navy blue "mercerized" sewing thread. Whatever that means. And a needle. And a pair of scissors. And a few loose bobby pins. What the hell. Take it all. Better to be safe than sorry. Meanwhile, I was banging my brain trying to come up with some kind of household substitute for an aspirator. Very important. A bulb or a flexible tube of some kind. If we had one of those kitchen gravy things it would be perfect....

But we didn't.

Wait a minute. Or did we? What had put it in my mind?

I hurried back to the kitchen and dumped my collection of obstetrical gewgaws into the stewpot. Getting crowded in there. Then I rummaged through the utensil drawers. Not much to rummage through. But by God, there, in a far rear corner behind a bunch of greasy potholders, was what I wanted. A glass basting syringe. Or maybe it was some kind of clear hard plastic—anyway, about five inches long with a narrow curved tip and a blue rubber bulb. Eureka! A pretty useless item to have carted all the way up here into the hills—Sharon hadn't cooked a roast in a year. But it sure would come in handy now.

I tested the suction against the palm of my hand. Perfect. I removed the bulb so it wouldn't melt and set the syringe in the simmering pot. The glass looked a little dirty, but the boiling water ought to fix that soon enough.

Well.

I sighed a satisfied sigh, picked up the book and was just turning toward the bedroom doorway when I heard Sharon beginning to moan.

HEXAGRAM 8

PI

UNITY, COORDINATION

*...Those in trouble will be drawn
together because of the accord between
those in command and those who
obey....*

During the next half-hour or so, her pains grew considerably more rapid.

One of the first things I tried to do upon returning to her side was to listen for the fetal heartbeat. The fact that I wouldn't know tachycardia from wax in the ear didn't faze me—but it provided a sort of negative exculpation when, as I anticipated, I peeled my cheek from her abdomen, having failed to detect a single teeny thump.

That didn't particularly worry me. I never was any good at auscultation. But to reassure Sharon I told a slight lie.

"I think I might have heard something," I said, "very faintly."

I stroked her distended stomach, letting my fingertips stray downslope into the fringes of her pubic hair. "Anyway, I can't really tell. I'm sure it's all okay."

Then, after warning her to let me know immediately if I was hurting her, I tried my first vaginal examination. I had to experiment with a couple of positions before finding the least awkward. I ended up tugging off my boots and kneeling beside her on the inside of the mattress, supporting myself with my left hand while probing with the right.

In spite of my manual familiarity with the more external bumps and folds of the feminine orifice, I really wasn't sure what to expect as I plumbed deeper. Then too, for all its supposedly clinical aspects, I found the operation giving me a hard-on. I'd never last as a gynecologist. Sharon's neat little furry brown pussy, even now, proved an irresistible attraction. But I determinedly ignored what was going on in my pants and reached into the dank hot cavern.

Sharon squirmed. I had to push harder. My fingers touched something. She winced and grunted almost immediately. I jerked my hand out as though I had been burned. Christ, who knows what the hell I had felt! A large wet mass, fairly pliant. But whether it was the widening cervix or the descending baby itself I had no idea. And no intention of trying to ascertain further. My hands were shaking and my tongue was dry. I had an instantaneous craving for a cigarette. My erection had subsided like a popped balloon. I crawled over Sharon and stood up and wiped the blood from my fingers with the towel that had been between her legs. So much for amateur diagnostics. All the reasons for abandoning palpation quick-marched across my mind: I didn't have a sterile glove, I might be inserting dangerous bacteria, I might cause injury to Sharon or the vulnerable babeling. Dent the brain through the mushy fontanelle, scratch the skin with a fingernail, jab out an eye. Unh-unh. So far everything seemed to be going okay. Let's not complicate matters. Just allow nature to take its course. I rolled a cigarette and smoked it hungrily.

Up to this point Sharon had been dropping off to sleep between pains. For the most part. At least that gave me comfort that she was able to enjoy some respite. But now the frequency of the contractions made sleep impossible. And she seemed more frightened, though she was trying not to show it, during the interludes.

Early in the pregnancy we had considered various methods of natural childbirth. The county hospital clinic, of course, was no help at all in this regard. Very disapproving. But Sharon's friend Anita, another potter who lived in the hills above Berkeley, had recently had a baby using the Lamaze method. "Childbirth without fear"—no, I guess that's a different one, actually. Dick-Read. Grantly Dick-Read. Oddly named English obstetrician who was a big advocate of childbirth without drugs and such. They're almost the same, though, the methods. At any rate, Anita was now a great advocate of the Lamaze school—so-called after its French physician popularizer. She had pressed on Sharon several books explaining the Lamaze tenets, which Sharon had read with interest. (I, in line with my theory of Fatal misprision, had refused to give them more than a cursory riffle.) However, a requirement of the Lamaze method was attendance at a series of classes in which prospective mothers exercised to limber their pelvic muscles and learned to breathe in certain ways which, according to the claims of proponents, could, if performed properly, entirely eliminate pain during the birth process.

For several reasons—lack of money, geographical remove, reservations on my part (the man is supposed to participate too in order to learn how to coach his woman; that doesn't seem "natural" to me)—Sharon had never gone to any Lamaze classes. But she had scrutinized the books and experimented with some of the breathing exercises. Now, as a contraction would begin, she would start panting.

What exactly that was supposed to accomplish— except, perhaps, to keep her busy and distracted—I had yet to figure out. In fact, that was partly the basis of my quarrel with the Lamaze approach. And with hypnosis, another non-anesthetic method of labor analgesia. Technically one had been given no consciousness-dulling philter. The great experience of birth—of expelling a piece of your body which would now develop separately and mysteriously into a new and separate body, a peculiar human being—was undimmed. And yet it wasn't. Philosophically where was the difference between a hypnotist's psychic insinuations, or a Lamaze instructor's carefully coached Pavlovian breathing patterns, and a shot of chloroform? None was "natural." Spending six months in rehearsal, crawling about in leotards on the living room acrylic carpet practicing abdominal massages and transitional exhalations and expulsive contortions, was no more natural than a cesarean section. Less so, even. One of those monstrous modern perversions of a function which should be as casual as eating or napping or taking a crap. A pregnant woman is supposed to be out hoeing the corn patch and pounding acorns and milking the goats. *That's* her conditioning exercise. Then when it's time she repairs to her hut and listens to the shaman chant. That's your *natural* childbirth!

But, of course, it's somewhat easier to hold these fundamentalist views when you're male.

So I made no objections—far from it—when Sharon started huffing and puffing. We'd be engaged in vague, desultory chitchat—I trying to keep her mind occupied, she straining to oblige me—when suddenly she'd digress into a series of gasps. Rapid, shallow noisy insucks and outsighs of breath, like a winded puppy. And I would climb down from my chair and hunch beside her and begin to massage her thighs and calves. Telling my litany of exhortations:

"Okay, baby, okay. Just relax. Give in. Don't tighten up. Just let yourself go. Everything is completely limp, right? Your whole body. Just a sack of laundry. Completely limp. Right?"

And Sharon would writhe and groan and pant louder and faster... and gradually draw herself into a quivering bow... and then remember and start fighting to relax... and forget her panting and maybe sob once or twice... and then start panting again: "Huuh-huuh-huuh-huuh-huuh-huuh-huuh-huuh..." until she lost the rhythm and maybe choked on an extra mouthful of air. And I'd be kneeling there, madly pulping her muscles until, just as suddenly as it had swept upon her, the pain would recede. And Sharon would lie, flushed and trembling, floundering in the trough.

"Do you think," I asked after she had been at it for a while, "do you think that really helps any? That breathing?"

Sharon wasn't looking so hot any more. Or rather, I could see the effects of the ordeal on her face now, though in fact they had not diminished her beauty. Merely given it a different, ethereal, kind of *Dame-aux-Camelias* quality. Grey circles were beginning to be apparent under her eyes. The eyes themselves seemed sunken, glazed—and yet, for that, bigger. Her cheeks were wan, except at their crests, which were raddled unhealthily. Her lips were pale, almost bluish. There was sweat on her forehead and across her upper lip. She ran her hand over her mouth.

"I've always f...found breathing... to be a great boon," she declared.

Her unflagging impulse to hoist me by my semantic petard was an encouragement.

"Yeah, well you just keep at it," I said. I pinched her ass. But I was still anxious. She was shaking uncontrollably. Had been for about ten minutes now. Not with any particular violence, but steadily, teeth chattering. When she spoke she stuttered. It had to be plenty warm enough for her in here. So she couldn't be shivering with chill. Whatever it was, I didn't like it.

"Why are you shaking like that?"

"I d... don't know." Her tongue flicked out across her quavering lips. Her mouth rasped drily.

"Are you thirsty?"

She nodded.

I scurried out to the kitchen and fetched a glass of cold water. She worked herself back against the wall to drink. But her head was too low on the pillow and her hand unsteady. When she tried to swallow she choked. Water dribbled out of the corners of her mouth. I grabbed the glass away from her and dabbed at her chin and neck with my shirttail. Then I cupped her head and helped her to sip a few mouthfuls.

"Not too much," I cautioned.

"Why?"

I shrugged. "Well," I said, "you're not supposed to have too much on your stomach right now, according to the book." I shrugged again. "Actually, I suppose that's really more for if you're going to get anesthetics, I don't know. Except you're not supposed to have a full bladder either, when the baby's coming through. Why? Do you want some more?"

She shook her head. She was still trembling.

"It's all that panting that's doing that," I suggested.

"Why....?"

"You're hyperventilating."

"Wh... where did you get that?"

"I don't know. I just made it up. Sounds reasonable, though. Doesn't it?"

"Not t... to m... me."

"Okay."

I set the glass aside and drew the covers up over her legs. Sharon kicked petulantly.

"I don't want those. Too hot."

"Aye-aye, ma'am."

I peeled the blankets back and bunched them at the foot of the mattress.

"Sweater," she complained. "It's too h-hot t-too." She thrashed irately, twisting her head from side to side like a child in a tantrum. "I don't want it *on* any more! T... take it off!" She looked and sounded as though she were on the verge of weeping.

"Sure, okay, baby."

"Please, Roger."

I leaned over her, alarmed, and fumbled at the belt.

"Huuh-huuh-huuh-huuh...."

Now I realized what had prompted her weird affects. I shifted my attentions to her thighs. Slow, methodic massage. Sharon gripped her abdomen and breathed from the chest. At first through slack guppy lips and then, as the knot tightened around her uterus, through gritted molars. The gasps took on a new sibilance:

"Shhhsh-shhhsh-shhhsh-shhhsh....."

"Try not to clench your jaws, baby. You've got to let all those voluntary muscles go limp. So you're not fighting the involuntary ones. Right?"

She made some sort of head motion.

"Just let the pelvic muscles do their job. Pull open that cervix. Let 'em work."

"Huuh-huuh... uuurrnh, *Uuuurnh!*"

"Easy... easy."

"*Uurn!* Oh. God. *Oh!*"

The cries had forced her jaws apart. She renewed her panting. Now each breath was wrung from deep within. Wrenched to the surface in agonized laryngeal croaks:

"Hhrrurnh-hhrrurnh-hhrrurnh...." Tears matted her eyelashes.

"Okay. All right," I urged her on. "The contraction's just about past now. Sharon? Baby? Keep a stiff upper lip. Figuratively, that is, not literally. Just relax. You're doing great. Fabulously."

"H h r r u r n h - h h r r u r n h . . . h u u h - h u u h - nuuh~hunnnnnnnn...."

I could feel the fibrous bundles under her skin slowly soften. She let the pulmonary pressure blow off in a long sigh, swallowed stickily, worked her tongue and lips to squeeze up saliva, swallowed again, and then suddenly, in the middle of a huge inspiration, began to cry.

I rocked back on my ankles. I didn't know what to do. I was pooped. My arms and wrists and fingers ached from manipulating Sharon's tensions. I slumped there dully, watching the tears roll down her cheeks, the furrows ripple across her brow, the woe blubber out through her rubbery lips. Her nose was running. A shiny rivulet of mucus trickled into the groove of her upper lip. She was really a mess. Emotionally shot and shaking like an automatic washer on spin cycle. When it seemed she was regaining some semblance of control, I roused myself and wiped the snot from her face.

Then, for hygienic purposes, I undid the bottom buttons of my shirt and used the opposite, clean tail to blot away her tears. She let me minister to her. Still snuffling. I mopped the exudations from the facial hollows where they had collected. Even poked a chambray-swathed finger into each tear-filled ear. Her tumescent features shone when I had finished.

"It h... hurts," she sobbed. "I'm sorry. It just fucking hurts so g... goddamned much, Roger! I'm just going a... all to p... pieces."

"No you're not!" I insisted. I smoothed her eyebrows. "There. You're beautiful as ever."

"I'm afraid. I'm n... not sure I can... c... can stand this much longer. I'm scared. I d... didn't... I mean, I *knew*.... But... I d... didn't think it w... w... would be this bad!"

"Doesn't it stop in between? Like now?"

"Yeah. B...but...."

"How about the breathing, the panting? Is that helping? At all?"

"I don't know." She rubbed a finger under her nose and sniffed noisily. Despondently. We had some Kleenex somewhere. "I must not be d... doing it right."

"I don't think so either," I agreed. "I think it's making you hyperventilate. Which is why you're shaking so much."

"M... maybe...."

I remembered there were some tissues in Sharon's dresser-crate. I got up and fetched her a couple. She blew her nose.

"Do you think you can keep on?" I asked. In spite of the blasé, matter-of-fact front I was trying to project, I was plenty upset myself. It was very unnerving watching Sharon churn through one of these latter contractions.

"I d... don't have any choi... choi...choice, do I?"

"Well, I meant we could still go to the hospital."

"No we couldn't. N... no. N... no. Huuh-huuh-huuhhuuh-huuh-huuh....."

136

Whether or not she was huffing as prescribed, the throes were clearly beyond that sort of palliation by now. Sharon heaved and tossed beneath my restraining hands. She seemed to be trying to wedge her protuberant body into some sheltering chink in the looming wall of pain. Creeping desperately along its length in search of some cranny she could hide in. Panting and sniveling, wide-eyed with panic.

Although I was supposed to be massaging her legs, pretty soon I found myself merely struggling to hold her down.

"Loose, loose," I was urging.

But it isn't the sort of admonition that can be enforced. So finally I let her go. She rolled away from me. She flopped about for a moment and then lay on her side, groaning to the wall. Once again I was confronted by blood. It purled gently down the crease between her buttock and thigh. It made me nervous. I continued to worry her flank with my left hand, while stretching out for the discarded towel with my right. The white terry-cloth was piebald now. Huge patches of nap had stiffened with claret stain. I looked for a clean segment, found one and shoved it into the dark intersection of clefts from which the blood issued.

"Ruuh-huuh-huuh... ruuh... huuh-huuh... rub... *uuurn!* Rub... the small... huuh-huuh... small ... small of my back, Roger... huuh-huuh-huuh... *uuurn...* huuh-huuh... *uuuuurnh!*"

Hastily I brushed her sweater up and cupped my hands over her hips. I dug my thumbs into the curve of her spine. Grappling with the lumbo-dorsal fascia. Not a very effective way to fight fascism, though, I soon decided. I tried jamming the heel of my hand hard against her tailbone. Massaging the sinewy girdle in a tight circle just above the pout of her buttock-flesh. I pinned her down with my left arm, leaning my weight across her hip, and strove with my right palm against the caudal vectors tormenting her. Kneading, thrusting, opposing with my full strength her tendency to curl when the contractions reached their zenith.

137

It must have done some good.

"Phwoo-whoooph! K... keep that up, R... Roger," she stammered after the paroxysm washed over.

"That's better than rubbing your legs?"

"Mm!"

I squeezed her arm and then pulled her toward me. Rolled her on her back so I could see her face. It was bathed in sweat. The room was far too hot for the heavy cardigan. She had asked me to take it off. Now I did.

"Th... thanks," Sharon smiled. She reached for my hand, pressed it weakly and brought it to her lips. "You're being g... great, Roger. Just great. I c... couldn't... I mean I wouldn't kn... know w... w... what to do... without you here." She kissed my knuckles.

She was lying there naked now. Mammoth with child, beautiful, mine. I was almost overcome. Again love—abstraction—became concrete. Solidified in my chest. For a moment I couldn't breathe. Couldn't speak. Reaction right out or the pages of *Cosmopolitan*. This was it, I thought—the most basic earthly situation. The keystone in the arch of life. Two mammals, mated, awaiting issue. Sequestered in their forest bower. The female whimpering, frightened by the secret forces convulsing her. But sustained by an instinctive pride. Strong in the crucial generative role Nature has invested in her. While the male, me, stalks restlessly about their moonlit covert. Ruff bristling, fangs flashing. Moodily, futilely sniffing after the invisible agent of his mate's distress.

Yeah.

I swallowed and dragged flashing mind back down to its bodily connections. I bent and kissed her on the mouth. Not long, because I knew she needed air. Her lips were grainy, parched. In contrast to her streaming face.

I was burning up too. I whipped off my shirt. The sleeve pits and back were sodden. I crumpled it into a wad and used the pockets to swab Sharon's forehead. And to blot between her breasts. And to soak up the sweat glistening under her arms.

The dank, pasty hairs once again fluffed out. Silken rainbow wisps, catching the candleflame. Her musky scent added to my excitement. I tossed the shirt aside and leaned low. Licked her fat nipple. Ran my tongue around the limp hummock, teasing and sucking till I felt it elongate. Pursing my lips against the soft wrinkles. I imagined I could taste her colostrum. The last time, this, I would not have to vie with a suckling infant for the precious elixir. I pulled at her tit selfishly. My dick, predictably, stiffening. The stoop and the tightness of my pants made things very uncomfortable. I reached down and unzipped my fly. Fumbled in crotch and flipped penis free. It stood out taut, quivering with relief. Sharon's fingers were in my hair. Tousling, caressing. Oh, the scene was enough to make Krafft-Ebing cringe.

And then her fingers went rigid, and I had to extricate my head from a cradle turned vise.

HEXAGRAM 9

HSIAO CH'U

THE LESSER NOURISHER

*...Dense clouds giving forth no rain
approach from the western outskirts....*

I rubbed her tailbone as previously directed, but I couldn't see that it made much difference.

Afterwards I stuffed my prick back where it belonged and got up, joints crackling. I tried to flex the soreness out of my limbs. I was polishing a new idea.

"How would you like," I asked, "how would you like a pain-killer?"

Sharon's heavy, lucent eyelids fluttered open. She was shaking worse than ever. She hadn't taken the last contraction very well at all. The tip of her tongue darted across her lips. "J... Jesus!" she grimaced.

The response was ambiguous, but I pressed on. "And what would you say if I told you I could come up with one?"

Her eyes glittered warily. "What?"

"Well. Suppose I were to... back the car up to the house and leave the motor running and attach a hose to the exhaust pipe, see, and then lead it into this room...."

She snorted.

"...And then every time you had a pain you'd just suck in a big mouthful of carbon monoxide, see...."

"Oh, b... beautiful, Roger! What a genius! Thanks a bunch."

"No." I hooked my thumbs in my pockets and hitched my pants lower. "No.... But suppose I told you I'd been thinking ahead and I got some morphine the last time I made a buy...."

She shifted feebly on the mattress. "M... morphine?"

"Yeah. And an outfit."

"Where'd you stash it?" she challenged.

"Never mind. What do you say? Would you take that?"

She studied me suspiciously. Her right arm was

crooked across her breast, dimpling its fullness. Her fingertips rested in the vee of her collarbone. She scratched her sunburn.

"How about it?"

She licked her lips. "Unh-unh," she finally grunted, shaking her head.

"You wouldn't?"

"No."

"Why?"

"Because." She sniffed loudly and worked herself over on her hip, facing away from me.

"Sharon?"

"Wh... what would it do?"

"Well, it would make you kind of euphoric and drowsy, I guess. And pretty soon you wouldn't feel any pain at all. Or at least hardly anything."

"Then I don't w... want any f... fucking morphine!"

"Why?" I challenged. "You said yourself you were getting scared. And you weren't sure you could stand it much longer."

"I kn... know. I know. But I want to f... feel my baby." Her voice was rising to a wail. "I want to *feel* it! Even though it hurts. Roger, it hurts so goddamn m...much!" Her voice sailed across into tears.

I knelt beside her with a tissue. I dangled it in front of her race. She snatched it out of my hand angrily, wiped her eyes and blew her nose. "I j... just want this... this to be real, Roger. That's all. I d... don't want to be drugged. Like some p... piece of r... reproducing meat."

"Okay, baby, okay," I said. "I know that. I admire that. As a matter of fact, there isn't any morphine...."

"Fucker," she interrupted. She was too disconsolate to give the word an inflection of surprise. She probably wasn't. I hoped so.

"I was sort of testing you. But I have a third alternative."

"I don't want to hear it. I don't trust anything you say

146

now. B... bastard."

"I don't blame you. But this is for real. Cannabis."

She honked into the flimsy tissue. One time, as it turned out, too many. The paper disintegrated, leaving her with a fistful of sodden pulp and slimy mucus. A pretty significant distraction. I struggled to my feet and ferried the whole box back to the rescue. She cleaned her palm and deposited the resultant wad of tissues in the space between the mattress and the wall.

"I'm going to roll you a joint," I said.

"No y... you aren't," she snapped. "I won't s... smoke it."

"Yes you will. Why won't you?"

"I just said."

"Sharon, I agree with you a hundred percen...."

"Huuh-huuh-huuh-huuh...."

Brief interruption in sound while we experienced network difficulties. The trouble, I had long since conceded, was not in the set.

When the static faded I leaped up and constructed a thick marijuana cigarette. Sharon was really strung out now— twitching spontaneously as though her body were nothing but a bale of raw, charged nerve ends. I lit the joint, inhaling only enough sweet smoke to bring the ember to life. I hunkered by her shoulder and wafted the joint under her nose.

"Here you go, baby," I said. "Is ancient Chinee lemedy."

Sharon opened her eyes and stared at the sputtering offering.

"Come on. You sure as hell need something."

She made no move to accept it.

"Since time immemorial," I intoned, trying to sound like a passage recited from a scholarly treatise, "cannabis, the drug manufactured by drying and curing the... resinous leaves... of the female cannabis sativa plant, or flowering India hemp... has been used as a pain-killer. This mild, non-habituating drug...." I faltered. "Uh... is mentioned frequently in the lore, the medical lore... of China. As well as that of other ancient peoples. By whom it was often prescribed as an analgesic. Hua To, a Chinese physician....'

"Yeah, right," Sharon scoffed.

"No, really!" I declared, grinning at this plum of esoterism. "Hua To, a Chinese physician... used hashish in surgery in... 200 B.C. or something. No kidding. I read that. And, uh... until 1937 or sometime... uh... cannabis was included in the United States Pharmacopoeia. But then Harry Bullslinger came along and fucked everything up."

I had run out of inspiration. I shook the joint at her impatiently.

Sharon's blue-green irises flicked back at me. "You d... don't think it would be wrong?"

"Christ, baby, of course not! Would I be giving it to you if I did?"

"Maybe it'll make it worse."

"Just take a little bit. You can always do more."

She blinked hesitantly, then puckered and craned forward to suck at the twisted tip. The ember flared, and blue smoke tendrils twined around my hand.

"I mean, I think completely natural, undrugged childbirth is a wonderful idea," I expanded. "But there's no point in being masochistic about it. This isn't going to knock you out or anything. In fact it might not even help all that much, I admit. In fact...."

I wondered if it could actually enhance the pain sensations, as she'd suggested. Jesus. I'd have to put my faith in Hua To.

Sharon had been holding the smoke in her lungs. Suddenly she choked and erupted in racking coughs. I was afraid the volcanic fit might turn her off, but she quickly recovered and dragged in a fresh lungful of pot.

The way her body was consuming oxygen—even the excess I suspected she was gulping—she ought to be flying

148

high within a matter of minutes.

"Not too much," I cautioned. "Till we see how it works. But you know," I continued, "in a way this might make it even more *natural* childbirth than natural. I mean, think about it. Wow! The *birth* trip! You know how grass sometimes really etches an experience in your mind? With all its connotations and implications and little individual rhythms and harmonies and stuff, all very clear? Really burned into your memory? Jesus! This could be almost *too* much! *Far out!*"

Sharon had snatched the joint from my hand. She toked up again, her trembling fingers scattering a fallout of ash. Tiny black flecks settled and clung to the damp skin of her chest.

"Not that birth," I acknowledged, "really requires a lot of help to make it memorable, though, I suppose."

She sipped an extra drag, tamping it down on top of the first, lungs stretched to their fullest expanse. Her heart ticked visibly through the drum-taut skin over her sternum. Right where the womb-mound bloomed away from her ribs. Her nostrils twitched as scavenged smoke exhausted. Automatically she held the joint up toward me.

"No thanks," I demurred, halting my hand in mid-reach. "I think I better stay real straight. Don't you?"

She blew out her breath and spent a moment filling with fresh air. "Yeah," she gasped, "I f... forgot. You better!"

She took one more toke before the next contraction swept her up. I pried the joint out of her fingers and set it aside, where it promptly died. Then I did my back-rub bit.

"If I ever kneaded love," I sang, bending over her butt with a will, "I knead you now."

I wrinkled my nose at the boundless depravity that would lead me to vent such a malodorous pun. But Sharon, to my pleased amazement, began to laugh. Between groans. Which meant she was unable to pant. The result, in a moment, was a seizure of really startling guttural bursts. But somehow not scary or unpleasant. When the sounds once again began

149

to fall within the human range, I asked her if the grass had taken any of the edge off.

"I...," she croaked. She cleared her throat and tried again. "I d... don't know. I think...." She shrugged. Her voice had gone hoarse beyond repair. "I don't know."

"You think it's safe to finish the rest of the joint? Think it's gonna do you good?"

"Mm-urrnh-urrnh-mm!'" She coughed, recovered. "That... means 'sure.' Why not?"

"Whatever," I smiled.

I relit the yellowed inch-long butt.

The harsh weed-smoke would probably further irritate her larynx. But she knew that. I handed her the stub and got up to find our roach-clip. It was in the ashtray on my writing table—burnished brass tweezers, handle hammered into an ornate ankh-*cum*-peace symbol. The clamp still gripped the charred remnant of the joint I had smoked earlier. I scraped the old roach loose and came back to afix the clip to Sharon's dwindling cigarette. She was starting to look stoned.

"You know," I said, "the lovely thing about grass is probably not so much that it's going to really deaden your pains. You know, which is why I find it so easy to approve. In spite of all my loudly professed convictions about not tampering with natural processes."

I apportioned my weight between my two sore kneecaps gingerly. "Not that I consider this tampering. Or even really interfering.... But I mean, that's why I think grass is so beautiful. Except I wouldn't expect it to make too much of a difference in the intensity of the pain, Sharon. I just want to warn you. You know, not like a narcotic. Which is good, right?" I sat back on my ankles. "No. But the thing about it, probably... you know, I imagine... is that it's going to kind of transform your reactions. Which is pain-damping in another

150

way, right? You know, by changing your mental state. Make the pain something that isn't frightening and sort of secretly dirty, but a thing to be savored and appreciated. Part of the bodily... contribution... or function... I can't find the word... part of a chorus... anyway, role, the body's role in this whole complex thing of pooping a baby into the world. I mean, something really to be in tune with, like during a contraction your skeletal structure and your musculature are vibrating to some fundamental elemental universal note, which is....

"Eff-flat," Sharon said. She seemed to find that funny. She giggled.

"Hey. I'm getting into a poetic thought here," I frowned. "Don't distract me. Now shut up. Where was I...? Like a chord. Like there's a universal chord, that echoes in each particular little corner of the galaxy, whenever there's a baby being born. And the baby contributes one note, you know, on key if it's properly formed, and full-term, ready to emerge, and all in position the way it's supposed to be and stuff. The baby's one note... or one set of notes, you know, like the right-hand part. And the mother is another. Mother is another. Rhymes. Except she's actually two distinct sets of notes. Her mental attitude— her brain tune—is one, and her physical vibrations—almost literally—are the other. And anyway, so the grass should make you see that and feel that and know it's right to be a part of that. Right? Which changes the pain and kind of makes it pleasure. No?"

"Golly."

"Doesn't that bring a tear to your throat and a lump to your eye? The sheer overwhelming beautifanousness of the imagery?"

"Eff-flat," Sharon repeated. "The note that falls in the crack. I bet that's the universal note, huh? Th... think about it."

"Fascinating," I muttered.

"I just wish you were here in my place, Roger. S... so you could have this wonderful experience instead of me. You seem to dig it so much."

The roach was down to a microscopic blackened stub. Not really resembling its metaphorical namesake, but close enough to suggest the etymology. A crimp in the enfolding paper was clasped between the prongs of the holder. Sharon held the hot stub about a quarter of an inch from her lips and sucked noisily. Trying to draw in the last fumes from the guttering ember. Her eyes, crossed in concentration on the joint beneath her nose, were red-rimmed and venous, the wings of her nostrils glowed. Secretory membranes enflamed by the acrid herb.

"Is that true?" I asked. "Do you really wish you weren't having the experience?"

The roach had finally gone cut. Sharon had trapped the dying vapors in her mouth, and was determinedly swallowing them down. Recycling whatever wisps remained with little sips of air. Purging the last marijuana infusion of every mind-altering molecule. So she couldn't answer for a minute.

"I mean, that's kind of a dirty dig, you know."

She coughed up the smoke and chuckled. When she had regained her breath she said, "Don't be silly. Of course not, Roger. I'm stoned. Totally irresponsible. Completely unaccountable for my remarks. I love it. Love this big bulging belly here. Pat-pat-pat. Wouldn't you? Want to look like a pear? And speaking of pears, what about this pair?"

She cupped her hands under her full breasts, pushing them up and squeezing them together grotesquely.

"How's that for boobs? The milk bar. What more could a woman ask? Better than sixteen weeks at Eileen Feather. I mean, so it involves a little hurly-burly. Hurly-burly in the belly-welly for a while-y. So what-y? I'm in tune with the universe. Isn't that it? Hey, you! Baby-Boy or Baby-Girl! Cut it out in there! Yes you, you burly little curly. Quit fucking around with my cervix. Come out this minute! You hear me? I'm talking to you! No more of this brouhaha. Understand?

Brouhaha. *Brouhaha...* hahahahahaha...."

The word degenerated into a spate of uncontrolled, stoned laughter. Sharon let herself go. Soaring, dipping, zooming—ballooning aloft for as long as possible on this rarefied mental gust. After a minute I got tired of watching the unshared hilarity ripple across her bloat. I took the roach-holder from her hand and put it back on my writing table. I checked the objects boiling on the stove. Replenished the water that had steamed off, glanced at the fire to make sure it was adequately nourished. When I returned Sharon was earthbound again. Her eyes were closed. For the first time I noticed that she was no longer shaking. She was resting on her side, facing me. Her breasts were still freckled with fine cinders. I stooped and carefully smudged the flecks into the oily skin. Enjoying as always its pulpy spring. Sharon's mouth curved up in a tight little smile.

"Hey, love," I whispered. "Don't get me wrong. As far as I'm concerned, you're the undisputed Cosmic President of the International Sisterhood of Casual Laborers. And Queen of Local One. I have no desire whatsoever to trade unions. Solidarity forever."

I had worked that out in the kitchen. She rewarded me with an upward bob of the eyebrows. But immediately they plummeted. She winced, and her vocal cords began to rattle: "Nnnnnnnnnnh...."

I got down to massage her rump. Because she was facing outward, I crawled over her legs and knelt against the wall. She started to pant.

"Baby... why don't you experiment with not doing that for a while?" I suggested. "See if it makes any difference. You're not trembling now any more, you know? Have you noticed that? Maybe you can stop for good."

She gulped and nodded. She substituted a throaty monotone, with occasional glottal punctuations. These were studded in the middle with soft sharp barks—like voiced exclamation points. I toiled at her backside. The sweat oozed down my temples, dripped off my nose and seeped, stinging, into the corners of my eyes. As soon as I thought Sharon could make it without me, I gave up and collapsed supine at the foot of the mattress. I needed a moment to recharge.

HEXAGRAM 10

LÜ

TREADING

*...Though he treads upon the tiger's tail,
it does not bite him. Success!*

I reached over her knees, fumbled around for my shirt, finally pincered a wrinkle between my fingertips.

I hoisted the shirt across, stiff-armed like a crane, and draped it on my face. My sweat-soaked beard was too wet for the already soggy chambray to dry. The coarse blunt curls at the juncture of chin and neck itched ferociously. I scratched. Tried to blot at least that part of my beard thoroughly. I could feel pimply welts springing up in the track of my fingernails.

"Mmmmmm*mmm*mmmmmmm*mmm*mmmmmmm...."

Sharon was buzzing softly to herself. Varying the tone in accordance with some private pattern. The sound was leisurely and soothing, like a powersaw heard in the forest from a distance.

I lay limp, lulled by her hum, the shirt shrouding my face from the candlelight. I was on the verge of sleep. In fact I had almost drifted over when I heard Sharon mumble something.

"Huh?" I grunted.

"...Because it isn't centered."

"What?"

"Oh." She giggled. "Was I talking out loud?"

"Yeah. What did you say?"

"Nothing. Craziness."

I felt her stir beside me.

"I just had this really vivid image. Only it wasn't very pleasant. I was a big pot, being thrown on a wheel, going round and round... and getting fatter and fatter." She giggled again. "It makes me dizzy."

She lapsed into silence. After a few seconds I prompted her: "So what was so unpleasant? Being dizzy?"

She flinched, startled. "Oh. No. Uh. See, it.... I was just imagining... I was this big pot, or bowl, you know, fresh clay, on a wheel. Being drawn up into this really lovely, tall, beautifully symmetrical, curvilinear shape. Like some kind of fantastically delicate urn or something. Just, really, God... I don't know, it almost makes me want to cry. It was so... really beautiful! And I was doing the throwing, too. Very carefully. With my arm, I remember, down inside, up to the elbow... bringing the clay higher and pushing, so gently, keeping the exquisite precision of the shape. Pushing it out. And my fingers were leaving just this perfect, delicate horizontal tracery on the outside. So shallow it was almost invisible. But it was there, you know, perfect. Like some kind of Platonic ideal pot... was what it was. That's what it was. Only all of a sudden something went wrong, and there was that awful, sickening yaw, you know, when the clay tilts. Brrrr! And the lip... started to get all contorted and thrown off, and the neck began to twist and fall over. Ugh! Like somebody running a fingernail down a blackboard. That's what it always reminds me of. Uugh! And the whole thing began to disintegrate. Which meant it wasn't centered. Wasn't centered."

"Wow."

She fell silent again. I waited, listening, expecting elaboration. But there was none. Only the regular calm hiss of her breathing.

Pretty soon my mind wandered. Seized on the fact of her apparent new looseness. My shoulder was touching, barely brushing, the base of her calf. The hairs of my body gleaning intelligence from the least undulations of hers. Like tiny seismic sensors. I felt I could read out an entire kinetic profile of Sharon from this single point of probe. And what it said was that the persistent twitching and trembling of the past hour had subsided. Completely. Great. The grass must have been good for her. Relaxed her. Made her less tense and afraid. Except, this most recent imaginative flight bore at least some intimations of bum-trippery. Jesus, let's hope not. Urging the marijuana on her had been well-intentioned— but disquietingly experimental. I crossed my fingers. That's the kind of resolute action with which I come to grips with life's uncertainties. I smiled acerbically to myself. Sighed and found I was inhaling Sharon's unmistakeable bodily perfume. I concentrated on that for a while. Until a skewed mustache whisker tickled the inside of my nostril. I reached under the shirt-veil and scratched. Smoothed the bristles into place over my lip, training the ends away from the central part. I wondered what I looked like by this time. I decided I would get up and examine my face in the mirror. Only, decision and accomplishment were two irreconcilable items. I didn't have the energy to heave myself off the mattress. So I lay there, pinned by the weight of the shirt, until Sharon announced the onset of another pain.

When she was droning peacefully once more, I did totter onto my feet. I started for the mirror, but along the way noticed one of the candles was going out. It had been stubby to begin with, and now there remained only a scrap of wick in a puddle of green wax. To save myself the effort of replacement later, I pinched out the flame and unwrapped the cellophane from one of the reserves. It was a similar Mexican job, thick and red and lavishly molded. I had to wait for the green wax to harden before I could crack it loose. I amused myself by casting my fingerprints. Letting the liquified wax congeal on the balls of my index finger and thumb. I'm always fascinated by the sensation produced: An initial searing weld as flesh meets tallow—exacerbating tactility—and then a gradual muffling of sensitivity under layers of waxen callus.

I rubbed my thumb and finger together, working the slushy substance until it had nearly solidified. Just before they were cemented, I pulled my fingers apart. I grasped the thin metal rim of the candleholder. The surface was fluted, but I couldn't feel the indentations. A strange discordance between sight and touch. Although touch is usually considered the more reliable sense. Funny. My nerve endings had been numbed by their horny coating. Except that wasn't it at all, I immediately decided. In fact, almost the opposite was true. In spite of the intervening wax, I could still feel the slightest contact. It was as though the nerves had grown extra-excitable to make up for their handicap. They were even using the wax buffer as a kind of extension—translating its sluggish vibrations into approximations of the message that would have been quickly perceptible under normal circumstances.

Quickly perceptible. An interesting figure. Cuts right to the quick. "Quick" for rapid, "quick" for corium, "quick" for living, vital. Because I had just begun to wonder if there wasn't an analogy here between the wax on my fingers and the marijuana on Sharon's mind....

Before I could examine the proposition further, though, Sharon's voice piped up from the mattress:

"Rob, that last contrac...."

I wheeled. "Rob!"

"Oh." I saw Sharon's eyes open to a squint. "God. Roger, I mean. I know who you are." She tittered uneasily.

"Let's hope so."

Before Sharon and I met, she had lived with a guy named Rob. And as far as I could recall, this was the first time in the two years we'd been together that his name had ever slipped out inadvertently.

"Jesus, I'm sorry, Roger. You know, there's a lot of similarity...."

"Yes, isn't there?"

She swallowed whatever she had been about to say.

I realized the situation was pretty extenuating. But I was hurt. And as the alien syllable reverberated in my head, I was angered too. I felt betrayed. Here I was, getting all wound up and soppy and maudlin about this big birth scene. How it was going to bring us together so close. And here she's got some other guy in mind entirely.

I split the little wax discs off my fingertips and tossed them on the table. I banged the old green wax loose from the holder and spiked the fresh red candle in its place. Sublimating in brusque activity what I knew to be—or was struggling to keep in perspective as—a petty and unproductive emotion. I scraped a kitchen match across the tabletop.

"I was just going to tell you, Roger.... Roger.... That all through that last contraction I felt colors. It was weird."

"Huh!" I lit the candle. "Felt colors?"

"Yeah. Like... what do you call that? Kinesthesia?"

I blew out the match. "No. Um.... Well, in a way that's close. But I know what you mean. Uh.... Kinesthesia's sensing your muscles moving. There's another word. For when you see sounds and hear light and stuff. Christ, now I can't think of it either."

My vocabulary musings had apparently dampened Sharon's anecdotal urge. At any rate, she did not go further into the details I was expecting. About her... *synesthesia!*

"Synesthesia!" I announced triumphantly. "Mixing up modes of perception."

"Mm."

Well, fuck her. There had never been any secret about Rob. Still.... I didn't like to think that fond memories of him were what came floating to her brain-surface at a time like this. I picked up one of the wax fragments and stared at it. The shallow concavity bore my thumbprint. Irregular whorls spreading outward like ripples in a pond. Strange, isn't it? How everyone's skin is uniquely striated. A personal design— conferred at birth and further individuated by the creases and scars of life. No other human being could match this impression I had made. Or so they say. A kind of editorial caret there at the tip, for example: memento of some accident— maybe a carelessly slammed car door at the age of nine. For some reason I still remember that. Hurt like hell. Who knows what corresponding psychic scars one bears as well? Psychic cicatrices. Psychatrices.

"Nnnnnn. Roger...."

Lazily I held the waxen shell over the candle flame. Watching it shrivel and vanish.

"Rogerrrrnrnrnr...!"

Shit. I didn't feel like rousing myself from my reverie right now. Going all the way over there and getting down on my hands and knees and exerting myself. My joints were frozen and my muscles awash with rancid fluids. Hadn't I done enough? Didn't I deserve a rest too?

I gathered up the remaining loose shards from the burnt-out candle and piled them around the flame. I tried to pay no attention to Sharon's gurgles. She'd do it anyway, even if I were there at my post.

The green wax dissolved slowly, creating a muddy pool. The two colors didn't blend right. As the level rose around the wick, turbid rivulets burbled over the sides. Ugly stalactites, like warts—dark, malignant growths—disfigured the candle's acanthine embellishments.

I turned and went to the mirror. The corner was in shadow. The peering face I saw in the glass reflected my new mood. Some kind of werewolf. Mr. Hyde. All jagged hair and bristle and vulpine bead-eyes and yellow fangs. The image was as much in my mind as my mien, but still I was taken aback. I knew the hours without sleep would have exacted their toll. Nevertheless.

"Oh. Roger. It's like.... *Uuuurnh!*"

I glanced over. Before remembering I was ignoring her. For the moment, at least.

I looked back at my own face. Quickly regaining my customary fondness for it. The straight nose, the high brow, the expressive grey eyes. The latter were slightly bloodshot. The lids a little puffy. I rubbed them. I ran my fingers through my forelock. Then picked up Sharon's tortoiseshell comb and did the job properly. Dragging the tines relentlessly through the snarled thatch over my ears. A grass stem fell out. Reminder of the afternoon's nap. And the afternoon's zap. I combed the long locks into a smooth helmet around my face. Untangling the full curls that straggled down the nape of my neck. I curried my mustache and beard. The result was a great improvement. I was Dr. Jekyll again.

"Huuh-huuh-huuh-yellow-huuh...."

Christ. She was starting that all over again. The breathing....

And suddenly I felt a flush of shame. What a despicable character I'd been playing. Dr. Jackal, if anything—and I didn't even deserve the honorific *Doctor*.

I slapped the comb down on the crate-top. "Hey, baby," I called. "I thought we weren't going to be doing that panting any more." I whirled in her direction. "Hang on! Relief is just a swallow away."

I crossed the room, stepped over her legs and knelt.

"Oh, *we* aren't," she croaked.

I bent to her sacroiliac with a will. She was scissoring her legs back and forth. Indeed, the panting did seem to have been only momentary. She was breathing hard, but irregularly.

"You can stop...," she sighed. "You don't have to do it any more." She reached around and touched my wrist. "I'm turning a nice comfortable purple again."

"Purple."

I continued my massage. Mostly out of a guilty conscience for not having been there sooner, when it might have done some real good.

"What's purple?" I inquired. "You look pink enough to me."

She squirmed out of my hands and, with a grunt, capsized onto her back. She paused, marshalling strength, then worked herself over onto her right side. It took her a few more seconds to get comfortable.

"I'm sorry, honey," I said. I bent down until my face was level with hers. The endearment had surprised me; it was not one of my usuals. It rang falsely. I pecked her on the tip of the nose. Somehow that was even falser. I felt like an inept parody of a suburban spouse.

"Man, oh, man!" she suddenly exclaimed. The point-blank volume ruffled my eyelashes. "That is weird!"

I recoiled.

"Really far out, Roger." She opened her eyes and I could see the pupils flare at my unexpected nearness. "Oh!"

I sidled backwards, to a conversational range.

"I'm sorry," she murmured. "I didn't know... you were...."

"Kissing you," I said. "On the nose. Didn't you feel it?"

She shook her head distractedly. It was pretty clear she was hailing me from some distant plateau of consciousness.

"So what's so weird?" I asked, trying to maintain communications.

"Oh, man. The contractions! That's what I was telling you! First there's this little flicker, like off in the corner of my mind. Just barely catching my attention. Only... if I try to look over there and see it, you know, I can't. But I know it's there... just this glint, this suggestion of something light all of a sudden in the blackness.... Because I've got my eyes closed.... But then gradually it starts to spread, and I can feel it, too, sort of washing up over me, from down in the center of my body, where the baby is.... Radiating.... And see, first it's just kind of purply, but then pretty soon it starts to get lighter, like an indigo, and then cobalt, and then some yellow seeps in, so there's this brilliant emerald green... wow! And then, you know, the whole way through... yellow and orange and red. All these fantastically brilliant changes, right through the spectrum. My whole body sort or exploding with... pain, yeah... like the sun or something. But.... And it's funny. The yellow-orange, right in there, that's the worst. Really searing.

Even though the red is at the height. But there's something cool about that, though, in the red. Like you can already tell.... Or... except maybe the red isn't the climax after all. Maybe I'm just assuming in my mind there's a rainbow progression. 'Cause that's the order, you learn. Hm...."

"Gee," I said.

"I'll have to... hm.... I'll see if that's so on the next one."

"You're not... apprehensive so much any more? About the contractions?"

She had been gazing toward the foot or the mattress. Now she shifted her attention and looked up at me. Her abstracted smile broadened, focused.

"Hi, Roger," she grinned. "Hey, I apologize. For calling you... you know. Just a slip of the tongue. All it was. Really." She laid her hand on my knee.

At mention of the subject a dull, bitter taste irrupted in my mouth. As though some heavy, swallowed metal lay undigested on my stomach. I forced a smile.

"I love you," she said. "Just you."

"I know," I nodded. That didn't sound right. But, really, there *is* no satisfactory response.

"How much longer do you think it'll be?" she wondered.

"I don't know." I shrugged. "Not much, probably."

"I hope not. But it's okay. You fixed me up. I can go on for a long time now. And you're taking such good care of me."

I shook my head, stung. "For a while there I was taking lousy care of you," I demurred. "I admit it. I was being a total bastard. But I won't be any more, I promise you."

"I know you won't."

"Just relax. And if it starts to get bad again...."

"Give me a kiss, Roger. Okay? That's all I need."

I did.

"I love you, Sharon," I assured her. "You can call me any name you want."

She wrinkled her nose. "I feel awful about that. Don't remind me. Let's completely forget it."

"Forgotten."

She smiled. But then the lines around her mouth began to stiffen. "Nnnnnnggg...," she croaked. "Here we go again!"

She shut her eyes and clasped my hand tightly. "See you in a minute or soooo... ooomph! Uh! Time for another of those light-shows."

HEXAGRAM 11

T'AI

PEACE

*...The active, bright principle (Yang)
lies within; the passive, dark principle
(Yin) lies without—strength lies
within, glad acceptance without.
The Superior Man is at the centre of
things....*

I stood in the doorway, testing the outside air the way you dangle a toe in a swimming pool.

I had made up my mind to plunge, but I was dreading those first few seconds of immersion.

The darkness was thick with fog. The light spilling over my shoulders was absorbed immediately, long before it had a chance to reach the ground. It was strange seeing my shadow printed vertically in front of me on the passing air. I sniffed tentatively and felt as though I were inhaling some opaque, syrupy X-ray contrast medium. The frigid draughts raced down my windpipe, coated my bronchi and spread tingling into each tiny ramification of the flourishing lung-tree. The effect after a moment was bracing. I squared my shoulders and marched down the steps, tits puckering like the skin under a four-day-old bandaid. The fog snatched my breath back in steamy wisps.

I walked a few feet away from the cabin, unzipped my fly and pissed into infinity. I flexed my knees, experimenting with elevations and trajectories. For my artillery spotting I had to rely on the sound of the splash and the amount of spatter that reached my bare feet. After a couple of precautionary final flips, I folded my organ away. I love that euphemism. And *member*. "Today one of our members, Peter Dick Koch, will give an organ recital."

I zipped my fly and ran each foot in turn down the back of my pants. I went over to the corner of the house, reached underneath and dredged another beer out of the refrigerating water-tub.

Back when I had access to a daily shower, I used to

end each morning's ritual by screwing down the hot water tap and doing my own frenzied version of the dance of the mating stork, spurred by an undiluted torrent of stinging cold water. It was a mortification of the flesh that had much more to do with Spartan pride than Christian asceticism. Maybe it was the same sort of impulse that kept me outside here now, shoeless and shirtless, clutching my can of icy beer. I ripped off the pop-top and tossed the ring into the void beneath the house for later policing. I took a long drink, figuring possibly I could lower my interior temperature to the point where I would no longer notice any disparity with the exterior. I wanted a moment alone, away from Sharon's impending presence. Freezing my bails off seemed like one good means of distraction.

I took another drink and felt myself turning blue. Blue reminded me of Sharon. She was still babbling about colors. Well, at least the pot had served its purpose. Between contractions, which continued regular and frequent, she was drowsing placidly. Hallucinating a bit, but not, I gathered, unpleasantly. Just before I'd come outside she had announced that a chorus line of shrimp were cancanning across the room. Asked me if I had let them in.

I chuckled at the memory. Immediately the chuckles transformed themselves into a violent shivering spasm. Some beer even sloshed out through the narrow opening in the can. I lapped up the foam washing around the rim and wiped my wrist on the seat of my pants. I couldn't control my convulsions completely, but I was able to manage sufficient choreography so that at least the beer stayed inside its container. I was determined to spend another minute or two in this refreshingly arctic outdoor atmosphere.

So anyway, I was vindicated. The marijuana had worked. Sharon had stopped shaking, she was practicing some kind of deep rhythmic breathing when the pains climaxed, and she was tolerating them much better. Now the main question was how much longer would they go on.

I shifted my weight from foot to foot and assayed the night around me. Dawn should be cracking any time now, I thought. Sharon had had her first pain when she was fixing dinner—which must have been about six-thirty or so. And if it was maybe four or five now.... I counted off on my fingers. That meant she had been in labor for around ten hours. Except there'd been a good long hiatus in there, from just about when we started eating to sometime after I was asleep. Let's say ten o'clock, that was. So maybe *that* was the point I should really be figuring from. Ten to five. Seven hours. Which, I recalled from the book, is supposed to be the most *common* length of labor for a first birth. And even if it was ten hours now, the book said the *average* was thirteen.

Christ. Who knows how much time might still be left? How long could it go on if the *average* is thirteen? Of course, it could be worse. If that were the median. Maybe a lot of labors are really short.

The only thing was, Sharon's contractions were coming thick and fast. Had been for quite a while now. I was sure they were down to, at the most, three minutes apart. That was the trouble with not owning a timepiece. Never in recent memory had the flow of arbitrary units seemed so freighted with importance. The number of minutes from one contraction to the next. The number of hours labor had endured. If you thought about it, though, there was no reason for clock-time to take on any greater significance now. Birth has its own organic schedule. Labor will persist until the cervix is fully dilated. The child will depart the uterus and emerge at its proper pace. Eight hours or twenty-four—what difference does it make? The Grand Design will be embroidered with its intended stitchery.

Except, again. Except it doesn't always work out that simply. Which was what was nagging at me. Even the chronometry has a rationale I had to acknowledge. It's a useful diagnostic tool, as much so as the stethoscope or the thermometer or the electron microscope... a particular

175

obsession with me, that last—not precisely a standard item in the family obstetrician's satchel. But it points up—embodies—my infatuation with modern science. At root, I am a believer... an unquestioning worshiper before the shrine of science—especially its sanctum sanctorum, molecular biology. I find myself fundamentally convinced that when man is peeping at ribosomes and chromosomes and lysosomes and mitochondria he is somehow focusing in on absolute truth. And that rubs off all over: bacteriology, virology, biology, particle physics. Because they deal with the infinitesimal, all those way-out microcosmic research bags seem to be kicking up whiffs of the infinite. Smaller is somehow truer. Division: the logical route to the uncaused cause. And yet... in the end you always bump up against Zeno's paradox.

For centuries the four elements, the nine qualities, the four humors, the four members... there's that word again... the three faculties, the two operations, the three spirits, the six non-naturals and the three contra-naturals added up to a reasonable and sufficient foundation for medico-scientific thought. Electron microscopy and the processes it depicts are no less constructs of the human mind than Galen's Pythagorean numerology. The only reason one has supplanted the other is that it produces better results. Vaccination saves more lives than blood-letting. But that doesn't mean that both won't, from some future vista-point, seem equally archaic. Achilles is not going to gain that last step on the tortoise just because a beam of theoretical particles and a finely-ground lens are trained on the gap.

So what it boils down to is that I suffer from... let's term it Nall's Paradox. An explicit distrust of the *"techne,"* coexisting with an implicit faith in the *"logos."* I believe that Nature is perfectly capable of blipping a baby out of the womb without any fourth-party interference. But I am also aware that She is just as capable of casually zapping both mother and child in the bargain. I, with all my pseudo-grasp of current knowledge about the physiology of parturition, have arrived at the same point as the savage who gapes in awe when the event commences. Stands back to let the kid claw and peck his way into the world like a hatching chick. We both figure the less intervention the better. On the other hand, I fully accept the idea that it is right and proper for the obstetrician—armed with his forceps and scalpels and anesthetics and sweep-second watches and occult metabolic insights—to step into the breach, so to speak, when the situation warrants. Turn a piece of wanton, anomalous—but perfectly natural — butchery into another happy—unnatural—vital statistic.

Which explains my unease now and throughout the night.

Like...

...I nipped at the beercan and swallowed a gulp. *Whooo! Fucking freezing!* My uvula creaked in the back of my throat— thick pink stalactite, now with an icicle extension....

...Like, I know the overwhelming preponderance of births will be normal and uncomplicated. But how do I know ours will fall into that fortunate category? Apparently the clinic doctor had detected no pelvic aberrations when he'd examined Sharon. And if he'd told her the baby had dropped and offered no further commentary... then I had to assume that meant it had settled into place head-first. But how could I be sure? A trained midwife would have been punching and kneading Sharon's blister-belly throughout this last seven hours. Figuring out exactly where the fetal forehead and chin and ass and limbs and umbilical cord were. Fingering her cervix and gauging everybody's heart rates and blood pressures. Acting responsibly. While I was just schlepping around in the dust with a second-hand high, sucking up beer and relying on the laws of probability.

Well, goddamn it, why not? We may not have been contributing to the advance of medicine, but we were sure as hell doing our bit for the psychic health of America.

Don't ask me, because I've forgotten, the formal rationalizations behind that statement. If any.

I'd been standing in more or less the same place, swaying from side to side at vague counterpoint to the twitches of my skin and skeleton. All of a sudden the dysrhythmia fell into some critical harmony—like the pawpads of the cat crossing the suspension bridge that set off fatal vibrations. I was rattled by a huge shudder that practically toppled me off my pins.

Movement, I decided. That was what I needed to keep the circulation going. Whatever happens, I reminded myself, I mustn't give in to sleep. Jack London and all. To build a fire.

I started walking around the clearing, listening for sounds of wildlife above the clacking of my molars. Since I believed that dawn was in the offing, I expected birds to start cheeping any moment. But the fog effectively dampened any noises I might have heard. I would almost have sworn the droplets themselves hissed and slished as they drifted over the mesa. At the corner of the house I stepped on a eucalyptus pod. That hurts! I stopped and massaged my heel.

The thing was, what if the kid's up in there sideways or something? Sharon grinding away in utter futility. Transverse presentation—nothing for it except cesarean. Or what if we had generated one of those reluctant types, too cautious to do anything but back out. The book had a section on breech deliveries. I was scarcely eager, though, to have to tug my kid out by the drumsticks. "Anomalies of the passenger," they called 'em, the doctors. Such picturesque terminology to cover such unlovely possibilities.

In 1500, Jacob Nufer, a Swiss sow-gelder, found his trade stood him in good stead when his wife ran into difficult labor. Herr Nufer made medical history by performing the first successful cesarean section on a living subject—his wife, whom he sliced open to deliver their baby after a dozen midwives and several barbers had failed. Frau Nufer lived to be seventy-seven and presented her husband with additional healthy children. I read that this evening while munching on an oatmeal cookie. I doubt that I'll ever forget it.

I limped back toward the stoop. It was too dark to venture any further barefooted. I couldn't have been more than fifteen feet from the cabin, and yet the candlelight in the windows scarcely penetrated to me. The whole world seemed shot through gauze. Some dim blurry low-budget art-film technique. Or as though my eyeballs had been smudged from excessive careless handling. Like a lens. Leica lens.

I could just picture myself sawing through Sharon's belly-flesh. Cursing and sweating over our dull-bladed bread knife. "Just grit your teeth, baby."

What we really needed was one of those *electric* carving jobbies. Make the whole thing a breeze. Click-brrrrzzz. Funny, come to think of it: Those medieval Swiss sure seemed to play fast and loose with their relatives. Wilhelm Tell *und Sohn*. Jacob Nufer *und Frau*. Must be symptomatic of some national trait. Phlegm. Stuffy to the point of emotional rigor mortis. I tried to hitchhike in Switzerland once. After about six hours a Frenchman finally stopped to pick me up. Traveling lingerie sales rep. Took me as far as the nearest railway station and advised me to buy a ticket. Said the Swiss would never brake because they didn't want to lose their momentum. Some profundity lurking there. He meant chugging up the Alps, of course.

Ever since I've distrusted neutrals.

I wondered if I was pulling a Nufer with Sharon. Working out my stony concepts of pain and birth and nature and fate at her expense. Well, maybe that's how significant advances are recorded. Supposedly the first non-fatal cesarean in America was performed by a frontier obstetrician whose own wife, again, was the guinea pig. Stretched her flat on a wooden plank and doped her groggy with opium. I read that tonight, too. "Frontier Obstetrician." Hm. Sounds like a sure-fire title. Like "Lincoln's Doctor's Dog's Last Litter."

The bothersome detail about both those recollections, however, was that they involved surgery. And unusual, dangerous, problematic births. In no way did I dig on presiding over one of those.

So how much longer should I let Sharon labor? Shit, how could you say? Three more hours? Four more hours...? Ten? Arbitrary units again—even if I had some way of measuring them. The only thing to do was to watch her carefully. Make sure she wasn't getting wracked to pieces. Hell, I'd probably be the one who'd wear out first. All that wrestling and muscling. Not to mention the mental tension.

More of my doggerel....

No, I'd give her a while longer, and then if nothing seemed to be changing I'd truck her down to the hospital. Sharon's no martyr anyway. This whole idea was as much hers as mine. And besides, it was always predicated on the expectation that birth would occur easily and spontaneously. She would't object to a hospital if it were to come to that. And neither would I.

But I'd been out here way too long.

HEXAGRAM 12

P'I

STAGNATION, OBSTRUCTION

...The omen portends ill for the Superior Man, but he must not slacken in his righteous persistence....

I leaped inside, slammed the door and sagged against the jamb as though the pursuing cold were likely to try to batter its way in after me.

The sudden warmth set my teeth chattering with renewed enthusiasm. I hugged myself tightly, a sensation rather like making love to a folio of sandpaper. The beercan in my fist was clearly intent on sabotage. I banished it to the kitchen table. I went around to the stove, fished open the red-hot stoke-hole cover—singeing my fingers—and shoved in a fresh batch of wood.

I hadn't heard a peep from Sharon while I was outside—and I was never that far away from the porous wall-slats. Nor did I hear anything now. She must have had at least two contractions during my absence... maybe three. So evidently she had been able to field them without any great moans or shouts. Nevertheless, I didn't mean to shirk my responsibilities indefinitely. I padded to the doorway and scouted the scene.

Candles all still burning. Their rich, turbid light pulsating somnolently. Sharon inert on her pallet in the corner. One knee up, a saucer-sized dark stain just visible in its shadow. Beside her, at a careless angle to the wall, the rush-bottomed chair I had been sitting on earlier. My discarded shirt trailed over the front rung. Next to the mattress was an empty beercan. A soggy homemade cigarette butt floated on the top in an amber scum of ashes. In the middle of the floor lay the childbirth manual, splayed open upside down. The section on delivery techniques was the place being marked, I thought. Yes indeed, this was a real antiseptic clinical setting. I watched Sharon again for a moment. Keenly. Making sure she was still breathing. Naked, she glistened like a peeled potato.

Okay, breasts and belly were undulating faintly. Anyway, she stirred.

"Hi," I said.

"Oh, hi. Where were you?"

"Outside."

"I called to you a couple of times."

"I didn't hear you."

"Mm."

I walked into the room and across to her. "I'm sorry. I needed some fresh air."

"Me too," she said.

I smiled. "Gee, that's too bad. Because I'm afraid you're just going to have to wait a while."

She made a pouting face. "Rat."

"How about if I just blow on you? Would you settle for that?"

"Not what I consider fresh air."

"No...." I burped softly and grinned. "But, so why am I a rat, then, darling?"

"You know perfectly well. Going off and abandoning me. In my hour of need."

"Five or six minutes, maybe. I'll admit to that. But not an hour."

"I said *in* my hour...."

"In your *seven* hours, baby. Would be more like it. I have certain natural functions which must be served too, you know. At some point."

She reached a hand up toward me, the fingers waggling playfully. They were aimed at my crotch.

"And what were Roger's natural little functions up to this time? A pissy-wissy? Or a shitty-witty?"

I winced, rolled my eyes and backed off.

The fingers continued to beckon. "Hold my hand, Roger."

"Not when you're in that kind of mood. You're supposed to be nobly suffering and dignified."

"Roger!"

Her voice was taut with appeal, and urgent in a way I had come to recognize quickly tonight. I stepped forward and did as requested.

"Nnnnh! I need you, *every* minute! That's whynnh... unh!'""

I had been careless in my grip. She crunched my knuckles. I circled her wrist with my free hand and slid the trapped fingers loose. I knelt, and as she wriggled I grabbed her hips. I leaned into the pain, trying to mash it. Purée it. The contraction lasted fairly long, it seemed to me.

"Do you think... you want... it's time for another joint? Is the grass wearing off?"

Sharon lay quietly. She had made no noises at those first few grunts. I watched a tendon twitch in the side of her neck. Finally her head gave some kind of responsive bob.

"Is that a yes?" I rocked up on one foot in anticipation.

"Nnh," she croaked. She cleared her throat. "Not yet."

"Okay." I gave her a pat on the fanny and stood anyway. "I'm just going out to the kitchen to get my beer, then. I'll be right here when you need me."

"Mm." She was temporarily out of it again.

I took along the empty that had doubled as ashtray. I dropped it in the garbage bag. I picked up my fresh beer and tossed off a swig. I glanced around. The water in the pot had boiled low again. There didn't seem to be much sense in keeping it going indefinitely. Just use up all the water and maybe crack the syringe or something from too much heat. I got out a potholder and hefted the steaming vessel off the burner. I cleared a space among Sharon's clay things on the table and set the pot there.

While I was stuffing the holder back in the drawer I took delivery on a message from my stomach. The substance, thrumming over the wires with dull persistence for some time now, was: Beer's okay, pal, but how about sending down a little grub to go with it? Except for the midnight cookies, I hadn't eaten anything since dinner. And breakfast hour was approximately upon us.

I stole another kiss of the hops and began to prowl in search of something appetizing. Unfortunately there didn't seem to be much that could be consumed without tedious preparation. I found a little steatitic rice caked cold around the sides of an aluminum pan. Bleeaach! That's probably what I would have got if Sharon were fixing breakfast today. Later for that.

I delved hopefully through the grocery sack from yesterday's shopping stops. Found tortillas... a possibility. There were two blocks of cheese. Cheddar didn't appeal, but maybe a chunk of Monterey jack? I fingered the cellophane, imagining a mouthful. No... somehow jack struck me as too oleaginous for morning. Which left me with the tortillas. And I crossed them off because, upon consideration, an unadorned tortilla would just be a bite of tasteless pulp.

So I was back where I started—either another round of oatmeal cookies or something cooked on the stove. Like, say, a nice scrambled egg. Wouldn't that be lovely? Soft yellow curds, mildly seasoned with salt and pepper. And a pot of strong black coffee to clear my head of the beer and grass. Jangle me awake for—and through—the long sleepless morning ahead. Good God Almighty! There was nothing for it now but an egg. That's the trouble with a vivid imagination. A nice plump white delicately speckled Grade A extra large fancy farm fresh egg. Expertly cracked against the rim of a hot skillet. Slowly the halves are parted, releasing the gluey eggmeat. Plop and sizzle in the bubbling butter. Add, maybe, a splash of whole milk. A sprinkle of salt, a twist of the pepper mill, a pinch of oregano. Stir with the tines of a silver fork and cook until firm but moist. Serve on a platter of Spode, garnished with a sprig of ranunculus. A cup of hot coffee—Jamaica Blue Mountain—simmering fragrantly on the side. Holy Moley! Muttered with an inward wail of despair. My knees had gone wobbly, my vision had clouded and my stomach twitched brokenly. Because we just—no matter how hard I conjured it—we just didn't have any eggs. I was doomed to disappointment. That's the trouble with a vivid imagination.

I drained the beercan and clanked it down on the table. I let the taste dissolve in my mouth before rooting a cookie from the crumpled cellophane. After all, oatmeal *is* breakfast food, I consoled myself—and this was certainly better than nothing.

I gave the cookie a baleful, *sanpaku* eye. Nibbled....

"Ro-gerrr...."

A small remote summons.

My name on those lips was beginning to pall. I drifted to the door.

"Sharon, baby," I said, "I was just about to make myself some coffee. You have to have me right this minute?"

Her mumbled reply was inaudible. From the looks of things, though, she was not yet *in extremis*.

"You can do without me, can't you? Just while I accomplish this one little item? Okay?"

She slithered diagonally across the mattress, her right hand protecting her belly as though it might roll away otherwise. She grimaced at me around her knees—a grimace, I interpreted, of assent.

"I'll be right there," I assured her. "It'll only be a second more."

I popped the cookie into my mouth and spun back toward the kitchen.

I went to the shelf above the stove and got down our coffee pot. I took off the lid, removed the innards and blew on everything to redistribute the dust. We don't make coffee often. I dipped about half a potful of cold water from the bucket and set the wet percolator on a back burner. The flame fizzed and sputtered in retaliation. I was spooning a measure of Folger's drip grind from its scarlet tin when a shout from Sharon electrified me.

"Roger! Something's happening!"

"*Whuf?*"

"...Feels different!"

"*Wha... gh?*"

I coughed violently, tears squirting across my vision as I choked at the lump of soft cookie mush that had slid through the portal of my recklessly gaped-open gullet. I dropped the coffee tin amid an explosion of grounds and leaped for the door.

Wham!

Oh-my-God-all-Jesus-mighty! I'd cracked my left three minor bare toes against the oaken table leg. The second time tonight! Oh Jesus. Whimpering, I bent and clutched at the brutalized throbbing sweeties—hobbled for an instant but not completely halted. My momentum refused to relinquish me. Like some giant wounded whooping crane I continued in graceless ballet through the door and across the distance to Sharon's side. One-legged, gasping, but still more concerned about my main problem—Sharon's problem—than about my podiatric future. I pulled up above her, braking and bracing against the wall with an outthrust hand. Apparently my bounds had dislodged the cookie plug.

"What is it, baby?" I gurgled. "What feels different?"

"...Pushing...."

"Huh?"

She was on her back with both knees drawn up and her feet planted wide apart. Her arms were stiff at her sides, fists flat on the mattress cover. An irregular flush stained her face and upper chest. She was breathing rapidly, worriedly, her lips sucked tight against her teeth.

"You have to push now? Is that it?"

She shut her eyes and nodded. Swallowed hard. Then shrugged.

"Okay. Calm down. What are you saying? Did you have an urge to push on the last one?"

"Yeah. I don't know." Her voice was weak. She worked her legs slowly. "I think."

"Okay. Okay." Carefully I lowered my damaged landing gear to the runway. "Okay."

"It's starting to come out now. I can just tell."

"Yeah. Right. Okay... oh... Jesus... um...."

Alarm had rocketed up from my chest, but I closed my throat and shut it in. Pinching off my voice before it betrayed me. There was blood. Puddling anew against the dam of her buttocks. And yes, I could see it, her pubis definitely looked swollen now. The lips beginning to part under the wedge of a baby head. At least hope it's a head.... Oh Jesus God...."

"Nnngggg...." That prefatory guttural tremor. The muscles girdling her womb knotted visibly.

All right. All right. Let's see, I thought. Keep calm.

"Nnnn... *uuuurrn!*"

Suddenly she *was* pushing. She had caught her breath and was forcing it, like a dead weight, a boulder, against her uterus.

"*Don't!*" I shouted. "Not yet!"

I squatted and grabbed her thigh. Dug my fingernails into the skin to get her attention. "Hold off... just for a minute until I'm ready!"

Automatically my left hand went out to the stained bath towel, which had drifted into a corner. I began dabbing feverishly at the wet blood.

No, the least of my worries. I flung the towel away and jumped up. Newspapers. No, the other towel, the clean one. Where...? Christ, no, wait. My hands were filthy. Sharon ought to be disinfected again too. I whirled—the motion confluent with my mental state. I was momentarily stupefied by the spin of simultaneous necessities. Only Sharon's rigid body provided a sensory anchor. I stared at it blankly. Her face was puckered with strain. God, was she still pushing?

"Phwhoooo.... Phwhoooo...."

Through trumpet lips she was blowing off air. "Phwhooo...." Regular, sonorous, humid blasts like a spouting whale. I realized it was her substitute release.

"Good girl, that's it," I encouraged her.

I swung back into action. Gave her knee a flick of empathy as I passed. Damn, the bruised toes still throbbed when weight was applied. I peg-legged wincing to the newspaper pile and snatched off five or six sections. The topmost nude chick-pic licked across my attention drily, meaningless as heat lightning. I knelt at the foot of the mattress, tore away the rolled-up blankets and shoved the newspaper sections under the sheet. Slid them as far as I could toward Sharon's butt. Patted the pages flat for comfort—a couple of thicknesses worth to protect the ticking—then dragged the sheet back over everything. Practical strategy. I wouldn't want to touch those papers after my hands had been scrubbed.

I hopped up, starting for the kitchen. Oh damn, the book! That was something else. I ran and turned it over. "Delivery of the Infant," read the subhead. The facing page bore a cross-sectional diagram of a uterus, with a hunched-up passenger inching around the cervix. Right place. I set it on its back. Immediately the pages riffled shut upon themselves. My teeth and lips formed a four-letter word. I squatted and tore through the pages until I found the drawing again. I pinned the book open viciously, a chair-leg stabbed into its spine. Then I launched myself toward the kitchen.

"No pushing!" I called over my shoulder. "Think you can manage?"

The question was rhetorical. I didn't hang around for

an answer. I grabbed the bar of brown laundry soap, sloshed half the remaining water out of the sterilizer pot—again carelessly fricaseeing my fingers on the hot metal—mixed some cold water with it in a plastic basin and lathered my hands. I scoured my forearms up to the elbows, abrading the skin as thoroughly as I was able without a brush. In spite of earlier washing, my fingernails were still edged with grey. I dug them across the bar of soap, then worked the caked soap out by rubbing my nails against the callus of my palms. The result was not perfect, but acceptable. Anyway, there wasn't time for perfection. I rinsed, looked around for something to dry with, spotted nothing clean and decided to let the air do the job. I held my arms up in front of me, wrists delicately flopped the way I'd seen the TV medics do it, poised to receive sterile gown and rubber-gloves.

"Are you okay?" I shouted nervously to the door.

I heard some indistinct sound which, because it was indistinct, evidently meant the affirmative. Nevertheless, this was no time for play-acting. I snatched up the basin and sprang for the outside door. At the latch I remembered I shouldn't touch anything. So I dumped the dirty water on the floor. I swished a little cold around inside the basin, jettisoned that and took a clean basinful in to Sharon. I brought along the pot of boiled instruments too.

At this point, I am chagrined to admit, the residue of my readings left me slightly confused. Although I did recognize that Sharon had now entered the second—and climactic—stage of labor, identifiable by her newfound compulsion to push the baby out, I was uncertain whether she would be experiencing a single prolonged contraction or a spasmodic series. As I trotted into the room, however, I could see that she was reclining much more easily then before. She turned her head to look at me with clear, if expressionless, eyes. She had one foot up against the wall, her sole wedged against a vertical strip of molding. It was a position that struck me as vaguely unusual. But immediately she lowered it, and carefully flexed both legs. She wouldn't be doing all that, I thought, if she were still gripped by a contraction. So apparently the pattern of advance and recession continued.

"All right so far?" I inquired.

"Mm," she nodded. She wrinkled her forehead earnestly and sucked in her lips. Her eyes, damp and coruscant, were huge.

"Hey, I love you, Sharon," I said. "You're really being great, you know that? Fantastic! Now...."

I set the pot with the knife, scissors and stuff beside the chair. I went to fetch a diaper and the unused clean towel I had been saving.

"Now," I explained, "I'm going to give you one last wash-up, you know? Just to make sure everything'll be okay. Okay?"

I spread the towel out under her legs, soaped a washcloth and scrupulously cleansed the insides of her thighs, her buttocks, her mons and lower abdomen, and finally her anus. The book had mentioned that care must be exercised to prevent rectal germs from entering the birth canal. So I discarded the washcloth on the pile of newspapers and substituted a diaper to delve into the outermost laps of her vagina. I had to be very gingerly there, because the baby's bulk was perceptibly nearer to the distending threshold. I rinsed and blotted her groin with corners of the diaper. Then, guarding the critical exit, I rinsed and dried the rest of her lower body.

"Uuh-oh.... Bathroom," Sharon haltingly announced as I was finishing. "Got to go. Really. Sorry... uunh... got to, Roger...."

"Sheesh," I observed. I fired the wadded diaper over my shoulder in exasperation.

"Not... uuunh... this minute though... *woe!* Uuuunh... *uurnh!*"

As the pain welled, Sharon weltered. She craned her

194

head far back into the rills of her pillow, knitted her fists and gnashed her teeth. Then slowly her whimpers transformed themselves into snarls. She started gnawing off chunks of air and choking them down. Suddenly, with an explosive groan, she clutched the sides of the mattress, hunched her shoulders forward and jerked up her head. The cry and the abrupt jackknife were startling in their ferocity. I could almost feel the breath-hardened lungs smash into the yielding diaphragm. At the same moment she kicked up her right leg and thrust it, jammed it, thigh quivering, against the wall molding.

"Easy, baby, *easy!*" I cautioned. "Not too hard!"

"Nnnnn*nnrrrnh!*"

The violence of her effort scared me. Her face was turning scarlet. Again I could almost feel in my own viscera her struggle to expel the offending foreign object—the immense impacted splinter of potential humanity—infecting her.

"Okay, blow off! *Blow off!*" I urged.

Blood, an awful sap-thick trickle, issued anew from the nascent wound I hovered over.

Sharon fell back snorting. Immediately she locked in another lungful of air and, like stretched rubber, snapped taut, rebounded, straining at the sides of the mattress, head and shoulders once more suspended several inches above the sheet. Its wrinkled tucks tore loose from the lumped stuffing and buckled around her. She began to slew sideways against the pressure of her upraised foot. The muscles of both legs jittered spastically. The ropy veins on either side of her -throat stood out, pulsing. Her cheeks and chest turned purple with uneven patches of subsurface blood.

"Attagirl," I incanted, "good girl, good girl." I rocked compulsively from knees to heels, knees to heels. My lying face was ridged like a basset hound's. I was scared shitless.

"*Nnnnnnnrrrrh!*"

"Okay. Okay. Okay. Now maybe you should ease off a bit. A bit, huh, baby? Right?"

"Nnnnn... *aaaagh!*" she cried.

I almost dissolved. I spat up my heart. *"What? What?"*

"Aaagh! Leg... oh! Leg!"

By the declension of her body I could tell she meant the leg braced against the wall. I still didn't know what the matter was, but I leaped for her calf, snatched it to my stomach and began a feverish massage.

"Aaaaugh. Oh! Cramp!" she groaned. "Christ!"

She continued to claw at the mattress, writhing as I worked the leg over—really mashing my fingers in there, like a guy trying to squush fresh fruit. There was no doubt about it—I could definitely feel a knobby knur deep in the calf where a smooth muscle-bundle ought to have been. Now I remembered having read that both legs are supposed to be adjusted evenly in the stirrups of the delivery table. Stirrups! Delivery table! Otherwise there can be unequal wrenching or spraining of the pelvic muscles. Luckily, though, I guess this didn't yet have anything necessarily to do with any serious pelvic problems. Because, come to think of it, the book had also said that cramps are especially likely to occur during the second stage, and can be excruciating if they're not attended to. So I attended like mad—and when I felt the burr dissolve I tenderly lowered Sharon's leg to the level of the mattress.

"There. Better now? Huh?"

I demonstrated the principle of the joint for her a couple of times, experimentally. I searched her face for signs of snags.

"How's that? You know, you shouldn't... okay? You shouldn't, really, probably... put that one foot up there on the wall that way. It throws you all off balance, your body. How're you doing?"

She was just slipping back into the range where my yammering could actually make some connection. She puffed and sniffled and rubbed a hand across her forehead and licked the sweat off her upper lip and tried to sort out the birds-nests of hair snaggled beneath her on the pillow. By now the bedsheet looked as though it had been attacked with an eggbeater.

"Need...," she gasped, "something. Need to... push on... something."

"Push on the mattress," I said. "Push down. Instead of out. Can you? Do that?"

I scurried around her on my knees, attempting a hasty readjustment of the bedding before the next onslaught. I tugged at the bunches of sheet trapped beneath her. The rough cotton snagged on her wet skin.

"Uh," she grunted, "uh."

Meaning...?

"You want some more pot or something?" I offered.

"Uh... unh-unh." She rolled her head negatively, emphatically.

"It's coming now," I mumbled, apropos of encouragement. "Won't be long."

I shoved what I could of the sheet-ends back under the mattress. The whole outfit had slid away from the wall.

"Hu-um, brother," she sighed. Her voice had gained in strength. I glanced up at her and saw she was smiling.

"Almost over," I smiled back. "Almost over now."

I scrambled to my feet and dragged the box of diapers nearer.

"My God! This is *so* much better now, Roger. Can't imagine!"

"Yeah? Great."

I had just realized I would have to wash my hands again. At least should. Every time I handled something new. And there wasn't any boiling water now.

"Shoo-whoooh! Wow. Yeah. I mean it still... mmm... like hell. Wow. Even worse. But that *pushing,* when I can push that's such a *relief...!*"

"Great, baby," I said. I dashed for the kitchen. I slung

the whole bucket of cold water—maybe four inches was all that was left in it—up onto a stove burner and pirouetted back out the door.

"You're sure you don't need anything? Any...?" I crouched before Sharon's euphemistically dubbed "dresser" and rattled through the meager supply of cosmetic jars and nostrum bottles stored on its bottom shelf. "What about going to the bathroom?"

"Oh...."

I found the plastic pint of isopropyl rubbing alcohol I had been looking for.

"You still have to go? Because I don't really... see how...."

I unscrewed the cap, dashed a little of the clear liquid into my palm, set the bottle on the floor and scrubbed my hands together. The sweetly ammoniac fumes made my nose twitch. "Because, you know, I really think it's more likely you're just feeling the pressure on your bladder now. From what I read in the book. Of the baby passing through. Not so much that you actually have to go. Relieve yourself. You think?"

"Mm. Mm-mm." A voiced shrug.

I jumped up and whisked the alcohol over to her. "Well?" I insisted. "What does it feel like?"

"I don't *know!*" she shot back. "Right this instant... no, I don't have that same sensation, I guess."

"I just think it was the pressure in the birth canal," I maintained. "The book specifically mentions that."

I knelt between her legs, unfolded a clean diaper and dampened a section with alcohol.

"This might sting a little," I warned.

I gave her vulva a second disinfecting and wiped away the blood. When I touched the jelly-pink inner topography, Sharon winced. I thought she was reacting to the astringency of the fluid. But within a couple of seconds she was grunting, and within a couple more seconds she was pushing.

HEXAGRAM 13

T'UNG JÊN

LOVERS, FRIENDS, LIKE-MINDED PERSONS, UNIVERSAL BROTHERHOOD

*...This hexagram indicates that
someone weak comes to power,
occupies the centre of the stage and
responds to the creative force....*

From here on in the reel of events begins an even wilder acceleration.

It is only through a great effort of memory—and a certain desperate splicing-in of illusions—that I am able now to separate frames, to cut and edit the jumbled scenes, to stop and focus on blurred details once so vivid... so vivid I was sure they could never fade.

Strange, isn't it?

We devour a moment with our senses, like cannibals slurping hungrily at the spirit of their soupmeat. We gaze, giddy with concentration, at some slide-thin specimen sliced from the career of our lives. As we pan across the instant, millions of brain cells soak up every tint, every shadow, every keylight, every meaningful and meaningless jiggle. No high-speed film could ever hope to match the grainless sensitivity of that mental emulsion. And so we clap the clappers, jubilant at our victory over time. Cut! Pop it in the can. Another fragment snipped from the endless saga of the present. Stored securely in the archives, available for rerun whenever we want. Just riffle through the index, select the proper reel, snap it on the spindle and settle back in the rocking-chair loges. Smoking permitted—the screening room is immutably private.

8, 7, 6, 5, 4, 3, 2... beep, slap, slap, scritch... title, dissolve... copyright MCMLXVIII... up theme... and away we go: reliving—in flat, flickering, disjunct but sufficiently polychrome and cinemascopic mode—some memorial clip resurrected out of fidgety tempus. *À la recherche du ton perdu.*

And yet, gradually, that tone is even harder to recover. What we counted on as thoroughly fixed begins, inexorably, to dim. The colors wash, the cellular gel is not, after all, so stable:

it cracks, evaporates. Four-star sequences catalogued for sharp resolution turn out to be only a murky dance of distorted shapes. Postures, faces, bodies, scenes undulate, tantalizing, behind impenetrable sepia clouds. Memory swirls in one long lap dissolve. And each carefully guarded, treasured cameo, when opened to view, gives off the musty stink of decaying celluloid.

Well.

Anyway, as you will recall, when we last looked in on our heroine we found her cruelly infested with a tumefic parasite and about to explode. Now, as the final episode begins, she turns to her companion, rams her foot into his belly and says:

"Nrnh!"

To which he replies:

"Oooph!"

...Sees white, skids wallward and leaves several thicknesses of kneeskin plastered to the inside wale of his corduroys.

The problem was that I had no backing against which to buttress myself. Sharon, in her single-minded urge to eliminate, had planted her right foot upside the wall-molding again... and her left spang into my solar plexus. I hadn't been expecting the blow.

Upon momentary resipiscence, however, I grasped her ankle, cushioned her heel in the palm of my other hand and levered my bulk against her outward thrust. I managed to find a tenuous purchase for my toes—happily, the good ones—somewhere along the baseboard. At least both Sharon's legs were at the same level now.

"Nnnngggaaaah... phwhooo... phwhooo... phwhooo... *nnnnnrrrrrrnh!*"

She was a symphony of barnyard sounds. Beaststück.

No, that's unfair, inaccurate... highly. She was a symphony, all right—raw, atonal, but not, as these feeble attempts at graphic rendering might suggest (even to me, I'm afraid, inventing them in retrospect), comic. Far from it. In fact, there was a kind of awesome, primordial dignity about each animal bleat. And I attended with the hushed concentration of a critic at a premier performance. Rapt in the pizzicato play of her body's gut strings. The finale was obviously nearing.

Lentando. The contraction eased.

Sharon had torn the sheet loose again, snatching at the mattress. The bed was in irreparable disarray. I patted down the blood-wet billows under her legs, poked at the towel.

"All right, now, baby. Everything's," I reassured us, "okay so far. No worries, no problems. Just take it easy."

"Nnkk," she agreed, dry-tongued.

"I'm right here. It's almost done now."

She licked the corners of her mouth. Her lips rasped mucilaginously.

I put her foot down. I rolled sideways off my knees and sat, waiting. I tried to void my mind. I stretched forward and plucked the book closer. The chair slid with it.

"War?" she croaked. She cleared her throat. "Thirsty. So dry."

"Water!" I echoed, understanding belatedly. I had already bounced alert, adrenal glands secreting. I blinked around, spotted the glass I had brought in earlier, still half-full. I scurried over on all fours.

"Nn. Nn. *Nn. Nnnnnrrrrrn....*"

I abandoned the glass. Scrambled back to the foot of the bedding. Received her heel and braced. She pushed. Blood bubbled. Coursed around the knobby anus. I realized there was no longer a channel between her buttocks. The bifurcated space had widened and flattened. The pubic growth no longer met her thighs, but stood away, an isolated tangled thicket trailing about a volcanic fissure. Narrowing from its triangular spread atop the lowest ridge of the rumbling central cone.

"Phwhooo... phwhooo...."

She relaxed the pressure against me for a moment. Then suddenly renewed it. I toppled off balance. Threw out a hand to catch myself but, instead of opposing her kick, pulled at the convenient ankle for support. I dragged her with me, off the mattress, before my shoulder thumped into the wall.

"Oh, Jesus!" I gasped, apologizing.

Sharon, still fighting down pain, began to sob in surprise.

"*No, baby!* No, it's all *right*," I pleaded. "You're okay, aren't you? I didn't do anything. Did I?"

She was making frightful noises. Her head lolled back and struck the floor, bouncing with a sickening hollow crump. Blonde hair flowed among the warps and splinters, swept over dust and beerstains. She had carried a huge corkscrewed fistful of sheet with her as she yawed. Now she tugged on it, stretching the rest of the fabric taut around her, shaped near its tensile limit to the contours of her body. She couldn't keep her breath but would splat it out, like a compressed balloon, then shrilly inhale. Her foot was still jammed into my chestbone.

"Easy! Easy! Easy!" I implored her. "Easy!'

The baby was going to be born. I was going to need both hands, and freedom to maneuver.

I seized her ankle, shoved it away from me. I grabbed the chair with my other hand and inserted it between us. I wedged Sharon's foot against the back leg, heel resting on rung, and jerked the plaited sheet from between her fingers.

"Here," I instructed. "Hold this." I wrapped her left hand around the front leg of the chair. "Now. Pull. Okay?"

It was a brainstorm of unusual fortuity. Conservation of energy—utilizing Sharon's own forces, canceling each other out, instead of immobilizing mine. I hadn't proved very stable a surrogate stirrup anyway. And it worked. I retracted my counterweight and the chair... breath of relief... held fast. Sharon's left leg, properly bent and splayed, locked against the rear chair-limb. While her hand, pulling sharply on the front leg, anchored it in place. Brilliant piece of work. I would admire it at appropriate length when I had time. Right now I hunched, like a catcher behind home plate, poised to receive delivery.

Balk. No sign of baby yet.

The sobs started spacing themselves out. Sharon began to squirm as though she meant to reboard the mattress.

"You're okay," I announced. Asking.

I realized I was probably expecting dialogue too soon. I circled around and helped her to straighten out. Get her head back on the thin pillow. Pull some of the wrinkles flat beneath her. Brush little tangled floorthings—toenail parings, lintballs—out of her hair.

"You feel all right?" I persisted. "I mean, you know...."

She nodded. Then, throatily, "Yeah."

"How's that chair working out?"

"Mm." Nod.

"Okay. Beautiful. We're all set. Here...." I got her squared to the walls again. "Whole lot of pain?"

Labored swallows. Dry smackings of tongue. She shook her head. "Unh-unh."

"How about some more of that water now?"

"Mm."

I crawled over for the glass. The water looked stale. Transparent dust particles floated on the surface. Shouldn't be anything really wrong with it, though, I thought. I swirled the water clear as I returned. I put my hand under Sharon's neck, tilted her head forward and helped her to sip.

"Mm," she said. "That's"—thick lip-lick—"much better."

I lowered her head to the pillow.

"I'm doing fine," she said. Pallid smile. "Aren't I?"

"You sure are, baby. You sure are."

"You too."

"Oh, yeah."

"It's not so bad, really."

"Unh-unh. Glad to hear *you* say so."

"You're being fantastic."

"Whatever."

"Nnnn...."

"Okay. Just... just... just...." I scuttled back to my catcher's position.

"Hhhhnnnnnnnnrrrrrrnh! "

I splashed some more alcohol on my hands. Rubbed them together absently.

"Phwhooo...."

"That's it. Don't wear... yourself...."

"Nnnnrhn!"

The book. Toppled shut again. Damn it! Get that place open. I reached under her crooked knee and fumbled at the cover. Creased unruly fucking pages. Find... uh... my *God!* Stopped, transfixed.

My God! My God! I could *see* it! I *could!* I could *see* it! Wet, curling, black... hair! *Hair!* A *head!* My baby's *head!*

"Sharon!" I screamed. "I can see it now! I can see the baby's head!"

Her groan rose to a sort of wail. Then trailed off. Almost post-orgasmic.

Just barely visible. A sliver of scalp. Under the bulging pubescent skin, below the fiery clitoris, between the viscid parting lips. Our baby's head. Fine lanugo growth, dark, slick. Black with blood and vernix. Emerging from the warmth. I could touch it.

But then receded. Ducked back. Disappeared.

"I can I can I... could could could could could *see* it. See it. I.... You? You're... okay? *Almost* now. It's almost over. Sharon?"

A head. Thank God the head. So.

But which way? Facing? *Which way?* Couldn't tell.

Doesn't matter. Soon enough. All right now. All right now.

"Now?" she barked.

"Huh?"

"Still? Can you? See?"

"Unh-unh. Unh-unh. Not...."

Naked. Legs split. Sweat pouring off her body. Spasmodic rest stop. I canted forward, made to soothe her blasted beauty with a diaper. Swollen lips, hollow cheeks, sunken eyes. Heavy precious woman's eyelids. Sweat sweet. Attar of life. Pain. Labor. Golden hair. Golden candle flame flicker, light like Spanish gold. Woman in labor. Bare before me. Bare beneath me. Bare breasts, bare belly, bare cunt. Bare bloody female body corked fast with hidden head. Cunt-hole, fuck-hole, birth-hole. Stopped stuffed with mystery head. Mystery child. Our child. Our baby. Prick? Slit? Smooth female vaginal dimple child? Soon enough. Soon to come. Soon to cry, soon to....

"What," she gasped, "'s it look like?"

I shook my head. "Don't know." I was unbuckling my belt. "All I could tell was...."

"Can you... now? See it?"

"No, baby. Not really. Just some... brown or black, I guess... hair. That's all."

I slashed open my zipper and dragged my pants down over my butt. Struggled out of the legs. "I'll tell you what I can see, don't worry."

"Hair." A congested chuckle.

"Mm."

"Dark hai... *hn! Hhnnn... nnnnrrrn!*"

I slung the pants away. Dumped more alcohol over my hands. Whoops. Splattering carelessly. Across bare loins. My scrotum shriveled at the icy slap. Then slowly sizzled. Mp. Sunburned balls. Accidental marinade. Simmer, grimace. Necessary to be naked, though. Both bare-ass for this, under

209

God.

I bent up closer. Screw-bowed on my pelvis, squinting, stiff with body English.

"Attagirl!" I urged her. "Unh! Push! Push!"

All bare-ass. All three. The basic trio. Mother, father, baby. Last arrives in animal skin. Others should be same to welcome. Only right. Buff before biology. Rawly reverent. Humbly human. Stripped to essence. Animal flesh. *Verbum caro factum est.* Man's but meat. *Verbum caro....*"

Flipping thoughts while her vulva flared. Incredible distension. Meat pie, hair pie, bursting with juicy life. Third from two. Good Christ! So weeply wondrous.

Strange voice, husky, crackling—mine: "Keep! Unh! Keep on! Push, Sharon! Push!"

And: "*...Hhhhhrrrrrrrnnnnnh!*" she bellowed.

"I can see the baby's head again now! More. More. Okay. Lots of dark brown hair. Curly. Lovely head shape. Fantastic.... It's coming. Coming...."

But: "*...Hhhhhhhhnnnnnnnn,*" she wheezed.

And bye-bye baby. Sucked away. Not quite so far. Crown still glistening through the parchment gash. Pubic garlands. Haloing escutcheon. Royal terminology. Crimson trapping. *Non ex sanguinibus, neque ex voluntate carnis....* Fuck St. John. Man *is* meat-stock. Best is basest. Soup base. Soul food. Chili con carne. No spirit save as spice of flesh. Just look at this holy mortal emerging morsel. *Ex sanguinibus et ex voluntate carnis.* That damn well *is ex Deo. Quod Deus rerum natura est....*

And, but, so... verbal burble. *Et, sed, sic.* Latin yet. Is thatavism Jung fellow? Fibrillations of an overcharged brain....

Sharon's lashes were gummy with tears. Eyes fogged. Chin a peachpit. Lower lip chewed to blood. Clamped under twin glinting beaver teeth. I reached out and caressed her jellowy jowl.

"Just relax, Sharon. Lie back and take it easy. It's almost

210

over. A couple more should do it." I smiled. "Hey. You know what, woman? You've got a baby between your legs. Know that? Just very coyly peeping out at me, but looks like a winner. A beautiful son or daughter. A beautiful baby."

Sharon moaned.

"No! Everything's fine! You're beautiful! A beautiful brave woman. Dauntless. Um. Indefatigable. Huh? And in about two or so more contractions, I bet... you're going to be a mother. So it's all practically duck soup from now on in. Right? I love you, Sharon. Know that? I love you."

"Roger...."

More vapor than speech. But suddenly I felt her hand. Rustle beneath me. Brush, touch my hanging hairy gonads. A finger against the damp underseam of my penis. Closing gently, momentarily about this nub of manflesh. And as though her gesture bristled with electricity, my viscera heaved and my higher functions lurched, slowed, shorted, switched to auxiliary power.

"My God," I fairly growled, "I can't *say* how much I love you!"

"You, Roger," she whispered. "You." But then her eyes narrowed for distance inward. "Tell me... again...."

"What? Oh."

I pushed myself up. I had been angling down to kiss her. An untimely notion—I could not possibly have accomplished it without plopping flat on top of her anyway.

"Well, uh... right now, like I said... there's just this tiny little circle of baby pate. About two inches. And, uh... with a lot of, uh, curling brown hair, uh, wet, you know...."

"Hhnnnn," she keened. Breath building.

"Okay, all right now, let's make it a good one this time. Really lean into it when I...."

"*Hhrrrraaaaaaaaghghnnnrrnhaaaagh....*"

"*Push!*" I echoed. "*Push!*"

And pileous rubber flesh stretched straining, yawning,

pliant headplug pressing, cleaving, bulging, oozing....

Christ, what process, concept, sense of squealing terror—Buddha calm?—raged there, *must,* beneath the riving skull?

And lubric blood bled vivid, greasy... vulvar membrane skin thinned, tautened, pulsing, parting epidermal layer by cell-shocked layer....

"Stop!" I shouted. *"Stop pushing! Just for a second!"*

I grabbed a diaper, clean, alcohol-daubed. Draped and through it felt my child's still birth-locked brainpan. First external touch. God! Gently holding back, restraining.

"Phwhooo... shhhhsh... phwhooo...."

Sharon heaved.

"Okay, now start again pushing. Easy as you can, just steady. Easy."

"Ooooonh. *Rrrrrrrrrnnnn....*"

"Little more."

No tearing skin. Okay. Okay. Rectum guarded.

"Little harder. Push!"

"Nnnnrrrn!"

Ringleted Napoleonic hairline... hairline!... slithering out to brow... God, brow! Forehead, downy... down, face....

Facedown! Means it's perfect! Right on axis, thank Jesus! So far. Should I help? Pull too?

"Keep on, Sharon!"

"Uuuuunnnh!"

PLIP!

Plipped out! Popped out! Right out! Whole head! Whole squinched, wrinkled, pursed-up infant prune face! Flopped free, dropped. Clunk.

Out!

And limp lolled, cheek, damp nib of flattened nose, tump, slumped against my guarding knuckle. Bowed as though to kiss my hand, left hand, cloth-veiled, tending Sharon's anus. Then slowly turned. Loose nod and roll away toward Sharon's left thigh as I reached to cradle. Fearful, shaking, blunt, rough, murderous weapon fingers. Gouge, crush, wrench, bruise.... Adult, could.

But, careful, slid beneath, found, felt—God!—tiny tender velvet earlap, wisps of wet fur, warmth of bathing birth slime. Life in palm. Lifting, propping this protuberant messenger. Intelligence. My baby's *head*.

"*Stop, Sharon!*" I screeched. Somewhere found a more manful calm. "Your baby's halfway born!"

"Hhhhhnnnnn...." Siren-sigh of emotion, relief.

"Look! Can you see?"

"Hhhnn. Unnnh." She struggled up on an elbow, palsied, feverish with exhausted effort, matted hair flailing loose around her, tumbling over eyes and gargoyle features....

"Don't push now!" I instructed. "Wait."

I pried a hasty finger between her nympha and the strangled nape. Feeling for the cord....

"My baby," Sharon gasped. A chop of amazed laughter rippling....

...Touched it! There, see? Tough elastic braided lanyard looped white taut across a rounded shoulder. Gingerly I fingerhooked and flipped it sideways, safe....

"Now push!" I commanded. "Can you? Push!"

"*Nnnnrrrrnh!*"

Newborn mushface cupped in cautious hands. Smothering? Damaging? Distorting ductile features? The book said hands on either side of jaw....

Christ, hope in sweat and vernix cushion.... Which way was I supposed to guide? Down? Up? Tug too? But....

PLIP!

Again one plosive shot....

Juggled fumbled football panic... snatch! Nab! Hugged in. Cradled, safe, dear swooning Jesus...!

Look! Kicking, squirming... ruddy, rumpled, dazed dwarf cosmonaut aswim in spacesuit skin.... Still capsule-hitched umbilically....

Ha*ha!* Ha*ha!* Wine-red nozzle there between the legs... mushroom prick with walnut scrotum.... Wow! Well-hung stud...!

And staccato coughcough... *waaaah!*
 Wail of life.
Spontaneous combustion.
Alive!
A boy!
We were three!

HEXAGRAM 14

TA YÜ

GREAT POSSESSIONS

...He who possesses much—supreme success!

He squalled just the way they're supposed to.

It seemed a dirty trick, but I worked a hand down, snared his slippery little ankles and gently upended him. The way it shows in the books, like a sportsman exhibiting a trophy.

He took umbrage at that. Understandably. Tough little mother—spinal reflexes apparently okay. He arched his back, drew up his head, clenched his fists and churned them pugilistically beneath his angry pug face. As though, if I blundered into range, he would punch me out. He'd seemed a bit blue at first, but his color was rapidly brightening.

Sharon had dropped her head to the pillow. Face drained, skin flatly papering bone, eyelids half-masted. I dangled her son nearer. She gaped, mouth slack, a hint of smile—awe, first maternal pleasure of recognition—flitting at its corners.

"Madame," I announced, "your heir."

"Christ," she breathed, the smile breaking wide.

There wasn't time yet for further formalities. I stooped and peered closely into my kid's busy orifices. Flared, florid, fluid with blind outrage. I tried to marshall priorities. I caught his head and lowered him to the towel between Sharon's legs. Probably should suction nose and mouth first. Memory had also glimmered of controversy: something about not severing the umbilical hookup too soon. Supposed to be sure all those vital protective placental juices—and blood supplies—flow out to the body.

So okay. I blotted his face hurriedly, then reached for the pot of instruments.

Yes! God damn it to hairy hell! The syringe was there,

all right, but the rubber bulb was still on the kitchen table. Fucking idiot! Could I leave my post? Had to.

"Don't move, baby!" I snapped. "Either one of you."

"Huh?"

I leapt up. "Don't roll around, Sharon! Gotta get something!" I dashed for the kitchen.

"What's wrong? Is something wrong?" Fear laced her tone. Of course she was floundering up on her elbow to see. The baby was yowling.

"No, no, no!" I screamed. I snatched the bulb off the table and wheeled back into the room. "I just needed something! I got it! Lie back!" I skidded in on one knee. "See? He's fine!"

"Yeah. Oh, yeah...."

I tamped the bulb down over the glass.

"Oh, he's beautiful," she soughed. "He's *beautiful! He!* I *said* it'd be a boy. Ohhhhh...." She collapsed, jet-assisted, as directed.

"He's ugly as a toad," I suggested.

The crying had subsided, some. Must have worn himself out.

"Boo," Sharon denounced me weakly.

"Kidding. Sorry, buddy. Only kidding. You're fantastic. *He's... fantastic!* You can have him in a minute."

I slid the curved syringe end carefully between sonny's naked gums. Made sure his tonguetip was forward and depressed. Not too deep, not gag-deep. Okay. Squeezed.

Brother! He loved that! Went off like a Roman candle. Jerked and spat out the glass and flayed the world with a full accounting of his woes at this series of betrayals. More to come, though. Flecks of bloody mucus speckled the inside of the tube. I clamped his head and stuffed his ululations right back down on top of themselves. Merciless. This hurts you worse than it does me, buddy. But it's for your own good, uh-huh, uh-huh. The nostrils proved, if possible, an even greater indignity. I had one hell of a little protest movement on my hands by the time I was finished.

Now came the part I was most apprehensive about. Actually snipping the living umbilical hose. I mean, here was a really irrevocable act—a slice of knife through human tissue. And, of course, it positively teemed with symbolic associations. Murderous papa. Deprivation of oneness with mother nurture, Mother Nature. You'll get a booby in a minute, kid. Some say it's even better. I can vouch for that.

I set the syringe aside, dipped into the pot. Choice of carving blade or sewing scissors. Maybe scissors would be neater. Ought to probably disinfect again, though, first, I thought.

I withdrew my hand, puddled it with alcohol, rubbed up. Heedful this time not to drip—haste makes painful baste. My unsuspecting victim took his infant ease. Arched by mother's legs. I glanced at Sharon's bruised birth-mouth, pallid cord protruding like an unhealthy tongue of exhaustion. Cracks or rips? I didn't think... no, none immediately visible. Thanks be. One problem fewer.

So mmkay. I fished the scissors—whoops, hot—from the pot. Abraham and Isaac. Angel voices unlikely, though. Not the same. Can't go through life trailing a shriveled placenta. Make it hard to wear clothes well. Other kids would tease, too. I clacked the blades a couple of times, nerving myself. Wait... strip the cord, I'd read. I pinched it between two fingers at Sharon's vagina, squeezed along the length forcing contents sonward. The rippled milkblue surface felt oily—hairlessly, unnaturally smooth. I was reminded of the sensation when gutting trout. Made it more impersonal. I snagged the cord about three inches from the baby's tum. Snipped. Yeep. Like cutting caoutchouc. Instant of resistance—then parting, severance. A tiny ruby bloodbead bloomed for freedom. I wondered if it hurt. Although, after the trauma of a passage down the birth canal.... I nipped the end tight, reached into the pot for the spool of thread. I spun off what I hoped was enough, folded about an inch of the cord-stub back on itself, bound the join with loops of blue mercerized thread. I wasn't sure that was the right way to do it, but I figured it should suffice. Better than a paperclip, anyway, I should think. I tied off the splice with a few occult knots. Perhaps, let's hope, propitious. Okay, kid, you're on your own. America's newest navel hero. Red, white and blue belly-button cockade cockily commemorating independence. I gave him a pat on the crown. He cried for lost dependence.

"What's happening?" Sharon spoke. "Where's my baby? I want to see him."

"You will. Coming right up. I just cut the umbilical cord... you know."

"Ohh." The tone was inflected with sympathy.

"I better wrap him up," I said, "so he'll stay warm."

"I want to see." She pushed herself higher, neck straining. Dilute cherry-ade trickled out of the cord remnant as she shifted. I picked a paperclip from the bottom of the pot and stopped off the leak. I reached around behind me for a baby blanket.

"Oh, he's tiny. Look. I wonder what he weighs."

"Hm." I hadn't thought of that. Would be interesting to know. Possibly important. Certainly a factoid central to birth announcements and future health assesments. I unfolded and spread the blanket.

"Look at his little hands and little feet. And little prick."

"Yeah."

"A whole little man. He's all covered with stuff!"

"Mm." Yeah, I should probably wipe some of that off, I realized. Vernix caseosa. Cheesy varnish. Hard to improve on that description. Looked as though he'd just crawled out of a vat of lard. Give me a chance for closer examination.

"I want to hold him. I want to hold him," she demanded.

"You can, baby. You will. Don't you think I ought to

clean him off, though, first?"

"I... guess."

I shook open another diaper. "How about you? Sure you're feeling all right?"

"Oh, yeah. It's so great! Wow! It's over!"

"Just about." God, I was amazed at her strength. "Why don't you lie back? Don't take any chances."

"No. Want to watch. You. He's beautiful."

"Maternal prejudice."

Hastily I mopped his eyes, mouth and cheeks. Not too successfully, but I was afraid to use alcohol. He threshed, lips wildly smacking, twisting—avid, apparently, to gum me. It wasn't revenge or defense, I realized. Babies are programmed to suckle that way. The buccal-suckle reflex. Your instincts are good, my boy—soon to be corroborated. I ruffled his topknot dry....

"He's blond!" Sharon exclaimed. "You said dark.'"

"Yeah!" I agreed.

Blond. And his head didn't look at all misshapen by the birth trauma. I could feel the fontanel, soft, diamond-shaped, like a bruise on a cantaloupe. Pulsing lightly to the pressures of discovery. Just hide and hair tenting brain from weather. Damn, another blond in the family! I grinned. "So I did. So he is."

I touched a finger, no bigger than a caterpillar. Curled, in fact, like a traveling inch-worm. One, two, three, four, five, okay! They crept around my giant thumbstalk. Each bluntly tipped with a miniature nail. Overgrown already, impressively scratchy. I ran the diaper up his arm, across two pinched shoulders, over the hummocky breasts. They seemed swollen slightly, almost feminine. I let go his hand and circled a clubby infant foot. I was groping for the other when I heard Sharon sharply inhale.

"What!" Instant panic.

She didn't reply. She let herself down. She lay flat

for second, eyes to the ceiling. Then she said, "Like it's... a contraction again."

Fucking shit!

Twins? Could it possibly...?

No. No no no. We'd know. We'd have been told. Somebody would have realized, heard two heartbeats....

"The placenta!" I cried.

Of course! Christ. I'd been devoting much too much attention to the baby!

I swaddled him up in the diaper hastily, laid him on the blanket, tossed the ends around. I started to hand him across to Sharon when it occurred to me that she probably shouldn't be encumbered for the next few minutes.

"Here," I said, "Move your arm, kind of...." I leaned forward and did it myself. I nestled the wiggly bundle between her right arm and side. "...Like that. Just kind of cuddle him right now, okay? You can nurse him later. Soon enough. 'Kay?"

Sharon twisted, forgetting her body in the drama of this encounter. Beaming point-blank love into her baby's wizened face.

The drama, unfortunately, was lost on junior. He continued to whine.

I couldn't bask in it either. I tried to summon the data I had stored about this third and final stage of labor. What came to mind immediately was a shred I could have done without: This was supposed to be the time of greatest hemorrhage danger—when the placenta breaks loose from the walls of the uterus. And with that memory came a surge of real dread... a briny choking tidal fear that Sharon would die. I saw her... the drowning image vivid... bleeding before me, her color draining, her slack womb slowly filling with the serum of her own life. Pregnant again, paradoxically, with Death... while I knelt helpless, unable to save her, criminally negligent... a murderer! Of girl friend. And baby son, maybe, too.

And then, as quickly as it had crested, the terror foamed past. I flushed it through, out, trying to believe, trying to believe, straining to believe... that there would be no complications. She didn't have to bleed. She wouldn't die. Everything would be all right. The chances were a million to one against a tragedy of that sort. The problem was, no normal scene could now be summoned with sufficiently offsetting dramatic brilliance.

I grabbed the book, flipped a page. "Delivery of the Placenta." I wanted to take refuge in the words, the clear printed instructions. I couldn't concentrate, though. Shouldn't.

I stared at, studied, Sharon's abdomen. Hollow, empty. Amazing. So much smaller. But still tumescent, flaccid, paunchy. I blinked down, letting my eyes forage at random in the thicket of verbiage. They gulped a sentence:

"...A basin is placed between the patient's legs to receive the placenta and accompanying blood...."

Immediate mnemonic flash. The tail of umbilical cord is supposed to be curled up over the pubis. I fixed that. But also sudden doubts to reinforce my lurking dread: We didn't have the right kind of basin... Sharon was too low on the floor to fit one under her anyway... even in bulk I wouldn't know how to judge excessive blood loss (the reason for the collecting basin)....

"Nnn," Sharon creaked.

The sound proclaimed an event but no particular pain or alarm. And I could see her uterus contract. Harden like a nut and bob up toward her middle as the abdomen flattened. I remembered something about massaging the uterus... or maybe it was *not* massaging it. Oh Jesus wailing....

I plunged into the print again. Thrashed uncomprehendingly to the end of the page. The typography was really too dense for this kind of browsing. Shit. Despair. I cast the book aside. My memory of what to do was adequate, I rallied myself. And at present the best thing to do was nothing.

I stretched to limber my back muscles. Rotated my neck. Took a deep breath. Sighed. My genitals felt hot and sticky. I reached down, idly peeled penis from balls, sorted balls in scrotum. Let some air circulate. I hunted and scratched after inguinal itches. When in doubt, masturbate. The Freudian thought didn't especially disturb me... but I lifted my hand. Doused it, scrubbed both germy hands, in alcohol.

I had been carefully watching Sharon's belly. The lower crescent remained firm, the gibbous upper flabby. That was supposed to be a sign. I rocked forward and placed my palm flat above her pubic bush. Testing substratal conditions.

"Does it still feel like you're...?"

...In the middle of a contraction, I was going to ask. But a sudden jet of blood from her vagina struck me silent. Was that cause for terror? And all at once I noticed too that the cord was moving. Lapsing out toward me steadily, like a furtive serpent. Okay. Okay! In conjunction, all were perfectly normal indications that the placenta was loose. Each specifically listed in my book. So. So.

"Sharon? I think the placenta's coming now."

"Nn...."

Slither of cord ceased. No further blood. I waited a moment.

"Hey, baby? Can you sort of spread your legs a little more? And brace your feet?"

"Nn...."

"I think you should push now. Help."

"Nn...."

"Hey!"

That got her. Jerked her out of her somnolence. My words had apparently been cooling their heels in some mental antechamber. She rocked on her buttocks, opened her knees wider, rolled her head to clear it.

"Okay. When I say," I said, "you push."

226

She looked at me and nodded unenthusiastically. The nod gave her the momentum to cock a quick glance at our baby. He was buried in the blankets, huddled deep in her armpit. He seemed somewhat more reconciled to the world now. Silent, anyway. Satisfied, Sharon sagged.

I used her navel for my reference point. I cupped my fingers around the loose flesh bagging her uterus.

"Now," I said. "Push out."

The hardened muscular void, rid of its contents and compact as a volleyball, is supposed to act like an internal piston. Drive the placenta down and out along the capacious vaginal cylinder. At least that's what it says in the book. I increased my pressure. Folds of fatty skin bunched up between my thumbs. Sharon's navel, for the first time in months, was parenthetical, I noticed. Meanwhile, more cord slid out. The end that was twined up over her groin slowly coiled on itself. Crept through the bloody brush until, like a mesmerized cobra, it abruptly swayed up and fell off.

"Hey," I observed, detecting what I was failing to detect, "are you pushing like I asked you to?"

She let one hand flop over weakly—drop off the edge of the mattress and lie dramatically still on its back on the floor.

"What!" I was awfully jumpy. If that gesture had been a fiberglass pole, I'd be the holder of a new world's record.

She grunted. "Can't."

"What's wrong? Is something wrong?" I hadn't seen anything to suggest trouble. But maybe she was hemorrhaging internally. Or maybe... Jesus... maybe... who knows?

"Does anything not feel right?"

I guess the trepidation she had inspired was unintended. Her eyes seemed to unfog. I could sense a reining in of recumbent forces.

"Uh... unh-unh," she said, shaking her head. She considered for an instant. "Don't think so. Mn-mn."

"Hey, well then, come on!"

"I'm exhausted, Roger."

"I know! I know! But, baby, there's only this one more thing to get through with and then you can relax completely for as long as you want! Right?"

"Mm."

"Yeah, so come on, then. Let's go. Push!"

I adjusted my grip on her paunch, corrugated it. Sharon made a face, clutched the sides of the mattress and began broadcasting. I suspected there was really more energy going into noise than effect, but at least she was trying. However, the effort could be sustained only for brief periods. Actually, more like semicolons. Ejaculatory phrases, after which she would lapse into a comma and recover from the stress on her colon. Oh, how clever.

After two of these bouts, though, a viscid gory blister began to swell through her cunt. It was a fearsome sight, I thought—somehow much worse than a blood-smeared birthing baby. Maybe it was because this represented... not life, but moribund, functionless tissue. When the first bubble appeared, too, I was afraid it was a part of Sharon's innards. A cave-in of the vaginal wall, for example—or worse, a prolapsing uterus. I experienced the immediate adrenal fanfare appropriate if that had been the case... until I determined that the umbilical stub sure enough terminated in this blobby pulp. I let go of Sharon's stomach, sank on my heels and gasped in relief.

Sharon was gasping for other, more physiological, reasons.

"Okay! Okay!" I exulted. "Do it again!" I bounced up. "The afterbirth's almost out, baby. Let's go. One more time."

Sharon caught her breath... feebly lost it in practically the same squirt. "Uuuhhh. Phwhoooph. Can't. Really...."

"Yes you can. Come on."

"No, Roger. Oh... mmmp...." She tried. "Nnnnnnnn...."

I dragged her belly-skin toward me, digging for

handfuls of viscera. The placental bladder bulged. I had been hesitant to pull on it directly for fear a piece might break off or something. That was supposed to be the big concern— making certain no fragments were left behind in the womb or the vagina. Could cause infection, delayed hemorrhage... problems, anyway. Ideally, I figured, it was meant to slip out on its own. But Sharon's whimpers didn't bode well for prolongation of the situation. So I grasped the cord near its root, continued to press on her abdomen with one hand while twisting and tugging very gingerly at the emerging mess. I didn't have to work hard, though. The afterbirth oozed free and plopped shimmering on the towel. Out.

"Eureka!" I yelped.

Sharon's tensed legs kicked limp. She let out a historic sigh.

I crouched and inspected the thing. Like a half-baked, gooey pizza, maybe. Placenta means *cake* in Latin. Everything always seems to get back to Latin. I stirred at it with my finger. A six-inch disc of watery dough, thin tomato sauce, glutinous cheese—loosely collected in a cellophane wrapper. Hardly appetizing. On the other side it was waffled... what the hell was the term for these meaty sections? Like pepperoni slices laid rind to rind. I reached for the book. Smudged a bloody thumbprint across the margin of the page. Searched....

"...Uterine portion is made up of individual...." Ah! ..."Cotyledons. Not infrequently, one or more of these lobes may remain attached to the wall of the uterus, or separate in the vaginal tract. The placenta must therefore be examined carefully to insure that it has been delivered intact. If a cotyledon is missing, the physician inserts his hand into the uterus...."

Yeep! I put the book down. Chin on knee, I squinted at our family placenta like a haruspex seeking auguries. Which, in fact, I was, since a need to plumb Sharon's plumbing would switch out the lights on my future immediately. But all of the...

cotyledons... seemed to be there, as far as I could tell. At least as I turned the glutinous organ in my hands I couldn't find any evidence that it was less than whole. No traces of an absent pepperoni. No bites out of the covering membrane. Actually, looked at like this it reminded me more of a rayfish: slimy, flatly amorphous, umbilical remnant the tail. Wrong color, of course....

"You want to see the placenta, Sharon?"

I held it out for her. "Looks like it's all there... here."

She eyed what little was visible without raising her head. I tilted it more toward her.

"Hm," she nodded, grinning up one corner of her lips dubiously.

I was afraid it might drip something on her. I put the placenta in the bloody towel, folded all together into a neat, if sopping, package. For delivery to the hospital. Probably best to get a professional endorsement to my diagnosis that nothing was missing. "One of our cotyledons is missing...." Another sure-fire title. To a tale with a somber ending. And....

But....

By Christ...!

By *Jesus!*

I slumped sideways, fell off my knees, bare butt cheeks flattening passionately against the cool wood kiss of the floor. I swung my legs straight and groaned at the joyful ache of unbuckling joints. Boosted myself backwards until I could sag against the wall.

Wow.

Sackman. A leering frazzle.

I allowed myself the leer....

Because suddenly it had hit me that this tale was at its end.

Well, of course it wasn't. Just beginning....

But the process, birth, the regular process... was over! There were no more stages to come! Nothing specific left for me to expect. No further expertise, preparedness, demanded of me. It was *over!*

I mean, sure, all kinds of hellish complications could develop. Mustn't forget that. Rap on plywood. But, even given the haphazard horror that is—after all—everyday life... this ending looked happy. Not somber—*happy!*

We'd done it! Delivered our baby on our own! Wow. Ta-ra-ta-ra....!

I clunked my heels together. Ow. Cracked my ankle knobs. Reminded me of my banged toes. I hoisted the foot closer to see. The nail of the little toe bore a purple halo. An even livelier aura wreathed the joint of the piggy that ate roast beef. Speaking of which....

I fought my way out of repose, back up on all fours. I crawled dutifully to the towelful of placenta. I set it aside on a mat of newspaper. I wanted to dig on my son some more. My boy. Tweak his toes, see if I could spy any pigment in his eyes, try to discern my own genetic contributions.

But first I had to make certain Sharon could safely be dismissed to the recovery list.

HEXAGRAM 15

CHI'EN

MODESTY

...Modesty brings success. The Superior Man is able to carry affairs through to completion....

I stooped and scrutinized her pussy.

According to my book, the possibilities of giving birth for the first time without splitting the perineum were almost nil. I don't really know how much concern that had caused Sharon... but I, since I scarcely felt qualified to do an episiotomy, had been forced into stoic acceptance of the fact. Any rents, I concluded, would simply have to heal by themselves. (Nice to be snug on the intellectual side of the issue.) After all, that must be the form treatment takes in other primitive cultures. Only maybe the reason all those lacy-lipped ladies in our sanitized hospitals get sundered by their offspring is that they've never had sufficient cuntditioning. Then too, they're usually gassed gruntless or else skewered into caudal paralysis. So they've got no control. It's as though the baby had to punch its way out through mashed potatoes, or Silly Putty.

At any rate, and for whatever reason, Sharon's lovely labia had survived the birth unscathed. They were enflamed and slack—the route from her vacant womb still gaping elliptically. But the juncture, the fourchette, was intact. I unfurled a diaper and, using alcohol, carefully daubed away blood to be sure.

"Does this hurt?" I asked.

Sharon must have experienced some sensation, because she stiffened. But she shook her head no.

Dried blood had caked in the bordering hair. I rubbed around it, trying to clean her up but not exert too much pressure. "Let me know if anything hurts you," I insisted.

"Mm," she said. "Did the baby tear me?"

"No. Unh-unh. No. I was just checking." I smiled. "Looks to me like you're as good as new. All set for the second one to come out."

"Ho," she gasped. "Wouldn't that be something?" She raised a knee and cautiously pushed herself over on one side. She stared down at the baby. "Oh, wow! Who needs two? Look at this little guy. Isn't he magnificent?"

"You're pretty magnificent yourself, babe"

"I think he's tired out right now. He's kind of resting. See? Gee. Wow. He is *so* beautiful! I can't believe it. Just think, he's only a couple of minutes old...."

"Couple of minutes into this Vale of Tears."

"Who do you think he looks like?"

I let her natter while I finished wiping the insides of her thighs. The alcohol should disinfect, I thought, and aside from changing the sheet—which looked like something left over from an automobile accident—I couldn't think of anything else to do. Keep en eye on her, keep dirty stuff away from the lower part of her body. All things considered, it seemed to me this had been a pretty antiseptic deal.

"Do you have any pain anywhere?" I inquired. "Inside your abdomen or in your vagina or down here?" I touched her yoni.

She gave my questions responsible consideration. "Well," she said, "I can tell all those parts have been used, that's for sure!"

"But there's no particular real intense pain or anything?"

She lifted her eyebrows, stuck out her lower lip. "I don't," she shrugged, "especially think so."

"Great!" I exclaimed. "Then let's have a quick fuck."

"Aaagh!" She toppled in a mock swoon. The shock wave rocked the baby. He burst into piercing lament.

"You fiend!" Sharon hissed. "You *pervert!* Ugh!"

She wagged a finger at me, pointed low, stiff with castrating menace. "I never want to see that nasty thing again! Get it out of my sight!" She lurched around and patted her child. "Hey, hey," she soothed.

I balled up the diaper and sailed it into the mounting pile across the room.

Sharon turned to smile. She knitted her brow earnestly. "You know, I'm only about half-kidding. Wow." She shuddered. "The thought of having anything inside me.... Brrrr. I may never take another shit in my life, either."

"Sounds unhealthy."

I crawled up by her hips. "Here, let me have one more quick look at... hm. Who? Whom? What's-his-name, here." I reached over her and snuck my hands under bundled junior. "What *is* your name, fella? Does he strike you as a Seth?"

Seth had been our primary choice for a male name. I had favored Cybele in the event of a girl, although Sharon... but that contentious point was now moot, eh? On one thing we had been unanimous—no name could be conferred in the abstract.

I lifted him to the outside of the bed and unwrapped his blanket. Sharon edged toward the wall to make space. I took a second to fluff up and double her pillow. I wadded it beneath her shoulder blades, against the corner, so she could see.

"Yeah," she said. "Seth...." Testing its fit on the tongue. When allied to this particular diminutive subject.

"My God," I noted as I turned back the diaper, "will you look at what the tiny bugger's been up to already? Shame on him."

Between his bowed legs, pasted drippily into a crease of the cloth, was an olive-green Rorshach blot. Reminded me, being literal, of a stool. "Hardly five minutes old and already he's incontinent. Premature senility."

"You dodo...."

"Seth, my boy, you're going to have to get control of yourself." Yeah, the name did please. "Is he Seth then, you think?"

"Of course he is. Doesn't he look like the epitome of Seth to you?"

"Sure." I brought the book closer. "Only," I mused, "I wonder what he'd have to look like, really, not to be...."

I fingered to the page I wanted, pinned the book open under my knee. Seth was, no question, an honorable name. Means "appointed" in Hebrew. Third son of Adam and Eve. Fathered Enos—whose name means "man"—at the age of a hundred-and-five or something. Lived nine-hundred-and-twelve years and begat legions of sons and daughters. World could use them in those days. What with cryogenics and organ transplants and clones and interplanetary colonies... well, good luck, Sethy baby. Your handle may be more prophetic even than we think.

I came back to the business at hand.

"Immediate Postdelivery Care," I read the subhed aloud, "Of The Newborn." Hm. "Okay, this," I announced, pointing to the shit-blot, "this is meconium. It is a 'soft greenish-brown mixture of intestinal secretions and swallowed amniotic fluid.' It's supposed to be be passed 'early and often.' Urine too. Indicates the pipes are unobstructed. Hm. I wonder if he's peed yet?"

I glanced at his wrappings to see if there were damp spots. None noticeable. I proceeded with my checklist.

"Well, he doesn't have a harelip, or a cleft palate, thank goodness. Tongue seems okay. Let's see... accessory lobes on the ears... eeew! Nope. Ears okay. Right number of fingers and toes. That's," I gave Sharon a pixie grin, "what, ten each? If I'm not mistaken?"

Her expression was pained. Her eyes had not left baby Seth. Slowly she pointed to him.

He'd taken the unsupervised opportunity to slide his foot through the meconium.

"Ah, you little...," I growled. I seized his calf—the whole length, between ankle and knee, fitted into my hand comfortably—lifted his foot and wiped it off with a margin of the diaper. While I did that he rolled his other leg into the stuff.

"I can see you're going to be a charming child," I sighed. I dragged the diaper out from under him, scrubbed his leg and bottom. I tossed the diaper away and returned to my checklist.

"Let's see... vigorous and sustained sucking movements. He's got those all right. Patent anus. Yep, we know that's working."

There was an item about checking heart sounds for murmurs. I didn't comment on that aloud. I could actually see his heart tick, though. He seemed to be breathing fine. Ribcage clamshelling lustily when he took in air to cry. Then he'd flush a ferocious shade. Otherwise, like now, when calm, he was a glowing waxy pink. So.

"Genitals next. Testicles descended...?" I bent and extended my finger toward his grainy puff of scrotum. "Cough," I instructed.

It was wit I didn't expect either of my audience to appreciate. But maybe Seth did. He responded to the situation, at least, in a way I wish I'd sometime had the nerve to at one of those abject fingerings. He pissed on me.

"Yow!" I yelped as his weenie fizzed from ambuscade. I jerked my hand back, but not quite fast enough. The urine sprayed in a wobbly arc, plashed on my knuckles and drenched the blanket. He immediately—I swear it—he crinkled his eyes and broke into a toothless, face-splitting ear-to-ear baby smirk.

"*Ha*ha!" Sharon laughed, then clutched her stomach, groaning. "Oooh! Aagh. Don't amuse me like that, you guys. Mmp!"

"We are not," I frowned, "amusing." I addressed a few mimed karate chops over Sethy. "Particularly you, you pencil-neck. Honor thy father!"

I blotted my hand on his blanket. "Guess that answers

the question about pee, though. I would have to say he's looking good in all the elimination departments."

I alcoholed the defiled hand. "Did you see the way he grinned? *That's* precocious, isn't it?"

"I'm sure," she agreed, venturing a shallow chuckle. She reached out and stroked his hair.

I resumed my quest for balls. Felt two. He started crying when I handled him. Can't say I wasn't sympathetic. I looked over his dicky... scratch that, his penis. There's a certain elemental majesty about the male organ, no matter how immature, which commands recognition from all other males. In fact, considering its proportion to the rest of his body, he was far better equipped than I. If everything grew apace, he'd end up prodigiously hung. Since I was also well acquainted with his hair-trigger potentialities, I approached his piece with added respect—from the side, like a cautious gunsmith. I examined the foreskin. Especially fascinating to me, being circumcised.

Now that, come to think of it, was a topic for soul-searching. Should Sethy be subjected to the same mutilation in the name of a dubious hygiene?

"Well," I said, "you seem to have a pretty virile specimen here, lady. Both his testicles came out to play." I wiped my fingers. "You know, one of the things we've got to decide very quickly is whether we're going to have him circumcised. Like in a couple of days."

Sharon nodded.

My attention flickered up to the nearby scrap of umbilical cord. I could find no fault with the job I'd done... except I probably should have put some disinfectant on it. Maybe a sort of bandage, too, if he was going to wee all over himself. I plucked a tissue from the box, soaked it with alcohol and molded it around the stub.

"Supposed to be easier," she said, "to keep clean?"

"What, this here?"

"Circumcision. Reason for it."

"Oh. Yeah, that's what they say. Or used to, anyway."

"Makes for a shorter fuse, though."

"Huh?" I looked up in surprise. "Really? You think?"

"Hey," she exclaimed, "you know what he is? Talk about that! Hey! He's a Scorpio!"

"Great."

"A stinger. Practically born on the cusp...."

"Hey, Sharon, whoa. What's this business about a shorter fuse?"

She was grinning wide. "I just now stopped to think what sign he is." As my question filtered unavoidably into its field, her grin turned sheepish. Finally she shrugged. "You know. What I mean."

"Indeed."

She was probably right. But that offered scant comfort. The implication was, to put it mildly, unflattering.

"Are you casting aspersions on my manhood?" I sniffed.

"Not you, Roger. No, I just mean in general. Here, let's not get into a discussion about that now. Hurry up and finish with my baby. I haven't even really held him yet."

I opened a new diaper, lifted Seth off the wet blanket. Gee, he was light. Again I wished we had a scale. That had to be the most important single reportorial feature of any birth: "Migawd, little Cooper weighed 34 pounds 13 ounces and he had six teeth and Myra was in labor for two months!" And here we didn't even know. "Oh, Seth... um...well, slightly heavier than a six-pack, I would judge." We didn't even know what time he'd been born.

"One thing, Sharon, you're never going to get a chart on him. Even if we do know he's a Scorpio."

"Why? Oh. Gosh!" She looked worried. "I guess that's so." It's the sort of thing that *would* worry her.

I set Seth down on the topmost third of the diaper.

Immediately I saw that I had a problem. Far too much diaper for far too little baby. Hm.

"You do put diapers on tiny nippers like this, don't you?"

"Sure. I think," she agreed.

"Yeah, well...."

I fiddled with the long end, bunching and folding it in various unsatisfactory ways. Then I tried putting Sethy sideways on the diaper. I had a vague idea of how it was supposed to look when done right, but I was impatient and not very analytical. Seth didn't care for the fuss.

"You're bothering him, Roger," Sharon finally observed.

"Good creeping Christ, woman," I replied. My voice betrayed some signs of agitation. I took a couple of deep breaths so I wouldn't scare the baby. "Okay. All right. How do you do it? Do you know? Could you do it any better?"

"Well... not like that, anyway."

"Beautiful. Mother of the Year."

"Just.... Oh, just sort of wrap it around him for right now. I'll figure it out tomorrow. Come on. He's hungry."

"Yeah... not that he's going to get much yet. Whoops."

Praaap. Out pooped another pinguid dollop of meconium.

"Holy cow, Sharon!" I complained. "For a genital Scorpio, this is the most anal character I've ever met!"

"Funny. Come on, Roger, change it." She was really crackling with impatience.

"We're going to run out of these things in about four hours," I grumbled as I whisked the sullied diaper from beneath him, "if he keeps it up at this rate."

"Listen to that little voice complaining. He needs a mother's comforting. Don't you, baby? Baby Seth?"

"He needs a good spanking," I countered. "Iron discipline. Beat some sense of bowel responsibility into him."

I gave him a hasty sort of mummy-wrap, working from

the legs up so that at least if he pooped again I wouldn't see it. Spare that fastidious urge. I tucked him into a clean blanket. He was raging full out now. Face all red wrinkles and chasmic mouth. Tiny fluted tongue fluting sorrow that soared past human pitch. In the upper register his squeaky cries set my teeth on edge, and in the upper-upper I'd have been baying piteously if I were a dog. Actually, it almost frightened me. Because he would void himself of air completely and then just lie there with his tonguetip soundlessly oscillating. I was afraid he was going to snuff himself right out on one of these cycles. But he always bit it off and sobbed in enough breath to keep going. Indigoing. Flushed purple. I conceded that nothing but a nipple could console him.

I noticed something, though, I hadn't seen before: In the middle of his brow was a deep raspberry flush — a kind of birthmark, I guess. It seemed to be a nexus of minute fibrillar bloodvessels. Maybe, I hoped, it would fade again when he was serene. Otherwise he was pretty unremarkable. His irises—which as far as I had been able to tell were just plain black—were buried now amid the facial seams. His nose was a caricature, infant-anonymous: low-bridged trifoliate putty-nub. His eyebrows were sparse, his lashes stubby and dun. His head was... headshaped. Ears... earshaped. Hard to read paternity into features like these. If you've seen one baby, I suppose, you've seen 'em all. The most interesting thing about him was his blond hair—and that had to be an inheritance from Sharon.

"Hey, *hey*, little Sethy," I insisted. "Cool it, man. Calm down. Baby-baby-baby...."

This wasn't yet my forte, placation. I rumpled the silky fluff over his forehead. Lower down the hair clung, still damp and dark, to his temples. He had long brown Orthodox sideburns, too. Lovelocks.

"Here. My turn now," Sharon coaxed.

"I know. Which side do you want him?"

She adjusted herself, rolling lower until her left breast settled, softcupped, into the sheet. "Just right like this is fine," she said. She rubbed her fingers quickly over her nipple. It sprang up, pink and moist and firm.

I slid Seth around, into Sharon's beckoning arms. She cradled him awkwardly. Licked her lips in nervous anticipation as she hugged him close and concentrated on the difficult first mating of pap and pipsqueak.

It wasn't the simple routine operation I would have imagined it to be. Mainly because of Sethy. Nature had cranked in an adequate preliminary program, all right: The instant his cheek brushed her breast he stopped bawling. I mean like right *now!* Click, shut down. It was amazing. But then he went into another kind of frenzy, a wild self-defeating yaw, the sort of thing that messes up the moon-dockings. He began to swivel his head back and forth, side to side, puckered mouth slurping noisily at his own instinctive imaginings, lips glissading off Sharon's teat in the very periodic mania of his eagerness. It was funny.

Sharon—literally, I think, tickled—giggled.

"No, baby. You've got to be more deliberate," she counseled. "Here. Here. Patience. Here! No. Darn it!" She maneuvered herself on her elbow, working to swing the point of her chest over her son's speeding mouth. A corona of sweat shone above her brow.

And then they met.

Infant lips still wet with the fluid of his mother's womb. Tender virgin bump of mammary flesh. I could see the force of his suction as the pigmented aureole itself disappeared into his pulsing maw. Sharon gasped... more a catch of breath. I felt an empathetic, perhaps apprehensive, tingle in my own arid tit. He couldn't have been getting anything except a little lo-cal colostrum. Still, he chomped with gusto.

"How does it feel?" I asked after a moment.

"It.... It doesn't hurt at all. It's pretty neat."

I sat back on my calves, odd man out, absorbing the scene. My woman, naked as a maya, sprawled on the birthbloodied bedsheet, suckling our newborn son. Somehow I always have to make flesh words.

I drummed on the floorboards beside me with both fists.

Incredible. Miraculous. Thank you, Fate. Thank you.

"In fact," Sharon said, "it's just about... the most... fantastic feeling, this whole thing...."

Her voice broke in the middle of the sentence. Her smile suddenly blurred. She bent her head over Seth, watching him nurse. A tear splashed through the candlelight on Sethy's busy cheek.

I noticed the morning light scrabbling at the grime on the windowpanes.

HEXAGRAM 16

YÜ

REPOSE

*...Action according to the law of
righteousness begets repose (calm
confidence); repose (calm confidence)
stems from righteous action.
Therefore, heaven and earth accord
with this law...*

Later that day I drove Sharon and the baby down to the hospital.

I padded the back seat with blankets so Sharon could sit with her legs out. She cradled Seth on her breast and let him nurse when he was interested.

I really had to steel myself for the trip, because the whole prospect of hospital policies and procedures was so dismal, such an antithesis to everything we had been striving for, and on the face of it had achieved, in staying up in the hills to have Seth. Still, I wasn't ready yet to make a total break with modern medicine.

And, of course, my worst expectations were fully realized. Instant snot. We were greeted, it seemed, with every conceivable hassle—even threats of legal action. They were going to institute proceedings, a social worker huffed, to take Seth away from Sharon because she was "unfit." I just kept doggedly insisting that it had all happened so fast I wasn't able to get her there in time. Nobody believed me, but I didn't think they could prove any different. And I guess, in the end, they couldn't.

Anyway, though, in retaliation—or what I considered retaliation—they confined Sharon to a ward-bed for four days. The fact that the cost was coming out of the county's own tax sacks was our single, minimal, satisfaction. The desiccated quinquegenarian queen who was chief of OB-GYN—as moribund a walking human being as I have ever seen—after haughtily informing me that I was owed no explanations, allowed as how he wanted to be extremely cautious about puerperal infection. I think he figured the recondite adjective would give me a well-deserved scare. One young intern—sideburned and with a few daring curls straying over his oxford-cloth collar—kind of sneakily befriended us, though, and he said the whole staff were pretty nonplussed by Sharon's lack of ill effects. Seth was given a bunch of tests—exactly the reason I had surrendered him into this enemy camp—but they did it in such a way that he simply disappeared into the hospital's bowels for a day and a half. Sharon was practically hysterical, and I was stalking up and down the corridors muttering about Molotov cocktails and pistol-whippings and armed abductions, by the time the floor nurse finally materialized. She dumped Seth howling into Sharon's lap, plunked a hot formula bottle on the bedside table, cracked the sort of smile that kills germs on contact, wheeled without a word and ankled silently off on her Enna Jetticks.

And, of course, the long interruption meant that Sharon's breast milk had stopped coming in. "Look at that poor little skinny thing," the nurses would coo, casting Sharon's open bodice a scowl and thrusting a supplementary bottle into her fist. "Give him this. He certainly isn't getting enough to eat that way!" they'd sneer. It wasn't until we took him home that he learned he was going to have to chug seriously at a firm human nipple instead of settling for the easy guzzle from a flabby perforated rubber dug.

He was recorded at six pounds seven ounces on admission. Length nineteen inches. He was perfectly healthy. The birthmark, we were told, was hemangioma simplex. It faded by the time he was a month old. Not being ideologues, we had him circumcised.

So now, having filled in those details, I note that almost five months have elapsed. It's March, and, though ponderous cumulonimbus are lumbering about the sky, I have wrestled my table through the door so I can sit outside under the trees this morning. The weather is seasonably chilly, but for the moment I am warmed by direct sunlight beaming through a cleft in the scud. My manuscript is at my sweatered elbow. The breeze kicks up every so often, so I have to weight the pages with my coffee cup. Right now there's a scant half-inch of sedimentous brown liquid at the bottom, dead cold. I am considering getting up and hiking back over to the house for a hot refill. Although I am trying to work seriously, to think clearly, this is not one of my better mornings. Seth, most uncharacteristically, awoke in the middle of the night last night and sobbed unsolaceable for nearly two hours. I suppose he had some kind of stomach ailment. Sharon only recently trained him to forego his one a.m. feeding, so she refused to offer him her breast. After a while I gave out. Got up and ganged in. We took turns stoppering his wails with his pacifier, blearily humming and rocking him while the other tried to catnap under the pillows. Result: I am disgruntled and easily distracted. I analyze my fatigue... and decide that, rather than the depletion, the emptiness, I would expect to feel, there is an incongruous surfeit: an increase in internal pressure, a stuffiness of the brain, a swelling of the eyes in their sockets. The diffuse mottled light bouncing off this page pierces deep into my puffy cerebral lobes.... Which is all very absorbing introspection, but not exactly to the point. I cite it to excuse any fuzziness in what follows.

Meanwhile, I decided to go for the coffee. I drink it regularly now, especially when I am writing. I just settled in my chair again and took a sip.

A large drop spilled on the line this sen

tence
(quite a different one otherwise) was to occupy. My pencil lead would trace only a damp "sen..." through the liquid, so I've picked up below it. The irregular march of words, and the asymmetrical amber stain (the blue rule beneath it has begun to dissolve) are esthetically displeasing. But I have already

consigned too many paragraphs to this page to crumple and recopy it. You will not, of course, be affronted by that blotch if the manuscript reaches print. But I have left the gap to convey a sense of immediacy.

You see, I, like you, have just finished reading—rereading—the foregoing chapters. The rhythms of the prose and its sequence are so stenciled on my mind that I need only the barest mnemonic brush with each page to bring out the impression. But I am constantly striving to get a feel for the whole. Like Gutzon Borglum clambering down off his scaffold to check Teddy Roosevelt's likeness. And each time I do, I find something missing. So I ask myself questions—and Sharon asks me questions. A few days back I turned over the manuscript to her.

"Okay, baby," I said, apprehension cavorting about my authorly countenance, "here it is. See what you think."

She read—no mean undertaking, snatches at a time between feeding Seth and changing him and scrubbing his diapers and cooking our meals and washing dishes and slumping disconsolately in front of her own abandoned creative work. And caterwauling at me and fondling her infant son and keening about what we were going to do when our dwindling money dwindled completely.

"Oh, gee, no, I really like it," she would blink apologetically when, as frequently happened, I'd find her dozing with my precious pages scattered in her lap. Last evening she finally finished it.

"That's fascinating, Roger," she smiled. "I really think it's good. Very good. Though why anybody would want to read it is beyond me."

She tapped the sheaf against the tabletop to align the sheets, set it aside and went off to attend to Seth's waking chatter.

Perhaps you can imagine how encouraging I found all that to be.

256

But later, while Sharon spooned chicken-noodle dinner into and around Seth's face, I engaged her in literary discussion. I cocked my leg over the back of a chair and peppered her with demands for elaboration until she could no longer equivocate.

You know what the first thing I got was?

"Okay, Roger. What made you write it?"

Wow. She really cracks to the kernel of the matter. And the funny thing was, I couldn't say. Still can't, precisely.

Oh, there's that bit about having some personal compulsion to make flesh words. Lots of husbands bristle with Leicas and Nikons as they scuttle down the hall to the delivery room. I, on the other hand, seek to distill the events in language. Where they get a packet of slides, I get an X-ray. Skeletal letters—alphabet bones—which every reader must flesh for himself. It has been said of our age that it is characterized by a need to filter all experience through one or another recording medium. We have to play back reality— somehow corroborate it through a mirrored image—before we can accept it as real. (And isn't it hard to adjust to life's teeming irreversible flow after a weekend's immersion in the video universe of instant replays and isolated camera views? Man's design for perception is so much more satisfactory than God's.)

I suppose McLuhan would say that media are simply extensions of the human senses, and the essence of sense is the impulse to bring it to bear on experience. I keep coming full circle. Make flesh words so that words can be made flesh. Use a sense because the essence of sense is use. Experience reality by making it illusion, then experience illusion to fix the experience of reality.

Screwy. As is all theoretical speculation. I wrote about Seth's birth to revivify it. An act of memory more permanent than memory. I also wrote about it from an analytic impulse. Peg that dramatic slice of life on the logical structure of language, then perhaps we can parse it. (Tautological again.) Spy the dim outlines of the emotional heart, the meaning, if you will—though, upon consideration, I don't think I will—the way the radiologist squints at his X-ray plates. But there are always little blurs, little misleading dust motes and spots of developing chemicals that may or may not affect the diagnosis.

For example, one of Sharon's more unsettling comments was: "The way you describe things is very realistic, Roger, but... you know... well... if you were trying to be completely accurate... about us... I'm afraid it just didn't happen that way."

"Really!" I exclaimed.

"I mean, on a couple of things... you're sort of confused."

"What! Where am I confused?"

"Well, like with the first time I nursed Seth. Right after he was born. For instance. He wasn't all eager like that."

"That's one of my most vivid memories!" I objected.

"Later, yes. The next day, before we went down to the hospital, in the morning. Remember? That was the first time he got so excited, and we laughed about it. But he was fairly tired out right after he was born."

"Hey, no. Really! Hell, you were still stoned. How can you be sure?"

She shrugged. Certitude was apparent in the way she cocked her head.

"But... now wait," I pled. "Think! He was just newly born and you were trying to get your nip in his mouth and he was squirming around every which way and glaping like a fish? The first time you nursed him? I'm sure it was!"

"Unh-unh."

"'Corona of sweat' and all? I wrote? My God. Here I've got it all down so explicitly!"

"Newborn babies don't have that kind of energy, Roger."

"My gosh," I appealed. "Hey, what about it, Sethy? You

remember, right? She's wrong. Isn't she? And I'm right. Daddy's right."

He semaphored his chubby arms and grinned at me and blew thick yellow chicken-noodle bubble-blobs that dribbled down his chin.

So there is no adequate resolution to that difference. And the more I think about it, the less secure I become in my own recollection. Perhaps I allowed the requirements of art, of drama, as I saw it, to retrack my memory. Conveniently collaborated until I am no longer sure, or cannot afford to admit, what actually happened. Which calls into question so much else about the story I am passing off as true.

But to get back to the central concern, the problem that obsesses me: What made me write it?

Well, there was a didactic purpose, too. Rather, purposes. I hate to admit that. Morals are so unfashionable. And yet, therein, I suspect lies the source of my unease. Somewhere in the basement, the bedrock, the mechanism of my tale (depending on how metaphorically consistent I want to be—anyway, I forget whether Mt. Rushmore or the X-ray machine claims rhetorical ascendancy) there is a flaw. A crack. A squeaky valve, a malfunctioning tube. What the hell, use them all. So let's start rummaging in the esthetic boiler room, the basalt, the gearbox, and see what we come up with....

First, prominent, there is the modish aim to *épater les bourgeois. Les hypocrites.* Lay it on the line about sex... about bodily apertures, appendages, couplings and secretions... about language ("There sure is a lot of shitty talk in there," Sharon observed wryly. To which I replied, "I think that criticism speaks for itself.")... and about the natural bloody beginnings of life. Transgress all taboos, then man will be guiltless and free.

When I was an adolescent, bellying up to a slab of supermarket beef at the family dinner table, I suddenly received the conviction that if everybody butchered his own meat we would put an end to the world's problems. War, poverty, racism—here was the key to it all. Underlying every major manifestation of cant and hypocrisy was this fundamental alimentary hypocrisy—the pretense that the viands we eat were not once lowing, bleating, bleeding, eviscerated moo-cows and sheepies. I had quite a snarling- match with my insurance-adjuster father, who had never been closer to a feed-lot than a Sunday afternoon's drive, and who thought my proposal was disgusting. Since then I have noticed that the "look-city-boy-where-do-you-think-your-steaks-come-from-bonk-whinny-stab-hack-ha-ha-now-how's-your-appetite?" is a stage every sincere young intellectual seems to go through. Jean-Luc Godard slaughters a living pig in full color on screen in *Week-end*. (At least I didn't get Sharon pregnant just so I could take notes on her labor pains. At least I don't think I did.) And sure, there's a scintilla of truth flickering in that proposition: The less connection a man has with the gore and the gristle of life, the more easily he can be convinced he's a machine-tool. So, yes, that's one of the ideas operant in my report on Sharon's delivery.

But, as we talked, I began to worry about another aspect—sort of the other side of the same coin... er, gear... er, stratum.... Anyway, I asked:

"Do you think there's too much emphasis on blood and pain and, you know, grunts and all? Does it go on too long? Is it scary? If you had never had a baby, say, and you read this would it frighten you?"

Because just the opposite was my aim. I had been trying to show that childbirth, while somewhat more effort and bother than taffy-pulling, was not the hideous degrading torture it is so often depicted as being. Was I successful? We had approached it from that notion, and come out on the other side with our ideals relatively intact. Still, I had to, um, tell it like... you know. Had realism—or attempted realism, anyway—undermined intention?

"Gee, that's something I can't really answer," Sharon mused.

"Well...."

"Just about the time I was getting tired of labor pains... reading, I mean, about them... you had me going into delivery."

"Yeah, but that's a question of art...."

"Sure, because that's what you're asking me, isn't it?"

"I suppose...."

Socrates, in *The Republic*, says that the virile young philosopher-guardians of the State should be exposed only to artistic models of the courageous, the temperate, the holy, the free. They should never depict or imitate a woman when she is in affliction, or sorrow, or weeping—and certainly not one who is in sickness, love or labor.

Well, I have clearly disqualified myself as a guardian of Plato's State (but then, I rather like to think of myself as an artist anyway, a job-description which in itself would earn me a subpoena to appear before Plato's Un-Republican Activities Committee). Nevertheless, not failing to acknowledge the mismatch, I would like to dispute Socrates. Female complaints—okay, sure, no man is going to acierate his character by specializing in roles that call for mincing and sniveling. But a woman in labor—one who, like Sharon, accepts it bravely and humanly—is, I would argue, a very paragon of the courageous, the temperate, the holy, the free. (Of course, my whole case would be thrown out on other grounds by Socrates, who maintains that there is only one sort of narrative style—the simple expository—that may be employed by a truly good man. I, wretch that I am, would be quickly condemned as the sort of unscrupulous character who, "in right good earnest and before a large company... will attempt to represent the roll of thunder, the noise of wind and hail... will bark like a dog, bleat like a sheep, or crow like a cock; his entire art will consist in imitation of voice and gesture." Jesus. Did he ever have me pegged.)

And how much celebration of self is there in my "art?" Subtle paeans to my clearheadedness, my coolness under fire, my competence as midhusband?

Truly, I submit, there is little substance to that charge. Boob that I am, I am pretty sure my boobitude flares like a beacon. (Score a point on that point, scorer, for Mr. Socrates.)

Nope, my nerve-strung ministrations only went to prove how little in the way of outside assistance is actually needed if everything is okay. And that's all right too, because it reinforces my theoretical bulwarks. In New Guinea, a woman retreats to the forest alone when her term approaches. Builds herself a tiny hutch and delivers the infant unaided. Next day she's back on the job, rooting for sweet potatoes. Mewling tad strapped across her breast. Scarcely a dent in the hard, shallow sweep of her life. On the record, I bet Sharon could almost have equaled that. Score some points for women in labor.

(While I'm at it, *Portable Plato* at hand, let me cite Socrates in defense of Sharon's emphatic nudity: "Then let the wives of our guardians strip," he says, "for their virtue will be their robe.... And as for the man who laughs (or, let's update that, rages) at naked women exercising their bodies from the best of motives, in his laughter he is plucking 'a fruit of unripe wisdom'.... For it is, and ever will be, the best of sayings, that the useful is the noble and the hurtful is the base.")

But, I protest too much. If my tale requires all this emendation, it's probably screwed up irretrievably. I could go on and on....

The grey clouds overhead have solidified.

They roll, sag, settle around the treetops. The wind's force seems to be increasing as the lane in which it is free to blow is gradually compressed. Bernoulli's principle, if I am not mistaken. The sharp wind-edge rips wisps off the loose cloud underbelly. I can smell the sea on the gale, and my mucous membranes tighten in the air's salinity. We're going to have a pretty good rainstorm soon. The constant blow makes it hard to write, because I have to hold down the page I am working on with the spread fingers of my left hand. Still, the corners fold back on themselves, militate against my traveling pencil. I am going to have to hurry if I want to finish.... No, maybe I should just allow the rain to finish things for me. Keep on until I am forced to flee for cover, then let that be that. Relinquish to Nature herself the power arbitrarily to delimit my art. There is, there, a certain pleasing element of internal consistency.

But make no mistake about it, as President Nixon would say. On one point I want to be perfectly clear. My hymn to the wonders of childbirth is not intended to encourage overpopulation. That was among Sharon's voiced concerns.

"You know," she said, "it does occur to me that about the last thing the world needs right now is another book telling people how great it is to have children."

I agreed. And I found it hard to come to grips with her objection, because I was suddenly absorbed in Sethy's efforts to avoid eating. His appetite had been satisfied, but there was still a spoonful of chicken-noodle dinner paste left in the bottom of the jar. Rather than throw it away, Sharon had frugally undertaken to coax this final bit into his mouth. It seemed a simple enough request: "Just one more bite, Seth. Come on, open up. Just this one last swallow." Trouble was, he didn't see it that way. In fact, he had his jaws clamped so tightly and his lips tucked so truculently under his gums, that a bloodless white spot glowed in the pudgy rille beneath his baby nose. Every time Sharon poked the spoon at him he would swivel his head away. And every swipe carried off a little more of the spoon's contents. It wasn't long before he bore a pasty Pancho Villa mustache, the beginnings of a runny Fu Manchu beard, and two clown-like yellow smile extensions arching out across his cheeks. Sharon carefully scraped it all back into the spoon and started over. I had to admire her perseverance. But, even more, I was amused and impressed by my son's four-month-old pluck. He had decided he was not going to eat... and he was not going to eat! It didn't seem to anger him, his mother's importuning. He merely refused to recognize the existence of that proffered spoon. Other than, with eyes averted, calmly to twist away from it. There was no question that an independent intelligence was at work there. Steadfastly asserting its individuality. More and more, especially, I think, in the last month, Seth has become a personality to me. At first he was just a kind of noisome clot of untidy flesh and instincts... a Platonic idea—"baby"—suddenly arrived with disquieting substance. Thanks to his presence I had no peace, no sleep, no freedom and no sex-life. And little if any compensating feeling of paternity. It was disappointing. I had always expected such a momentous verbal event as fatherhood to wreak some vivid change in me. I can remember stumbling around on the morning after Seth was born, dazed with fatigue and relief, staring down at my prickly naked shanks and whispering to myself, "I'm a father. I'm a father." I realized then that the term was purely legal. Descriptive, not incantatory. I was still the same spindly bearded, grimy, unshorn blot on America's escutcheon I had always been. Only my surname was somewhat further diluted and my future earning power subject to garnishment for child support. Where was the wisdom? Where was the patriarchal confidence and authority? Where was the love?

Well, strangely... watching Seth's twinkling, obstinate, food-encrusted face bob before me I began to experience an acute twinge of it. They have been getting more frequent these days.

I swung my leg over the chairback and went to the doorway. I leaned against the frame.

"How many children," I posed, "do you think you'd like to have?"

Sharon let the spoon fall into the jar with a clink.

Capitulating.

"You picked the wrong moment to ask me that," she sighed. She scrubbed Seth's cheeks gruffly with the end of his bib. "Or maybe the right moment."

"See, what I'm getting at," I explained, "is whether the experience of natural childbirth and the way we did it would make you satisfied to have fewer children, or whether it was so exhilarating that you'd want to repeat the whole thing over and over."

"Mm-hm. Well, give me a couple of years to think about it."

"What if we got married? Would that change anything?"

"What!"

"I just mean... that's a consideration. Maybe it enters into your thinking."

"Don't be silly. Now what made you bring that up?"

"Okay, okay. I don't propose to go into a long deep discussion on that subject right now. All I'm saying is, my argument to someone who suggested I was encouraging indiscriminate breeding would be that, on the contrary, I'd like to see an improvement in the *quality* of child-bearing. Then we wouldn't have to rely so much on quantity, maybe."

"That's reasonably deft," she nodded. "I'll buy it, I guess."

I picked up a cleanish rag from the table, dipped it in water and came around to wipe off Seth's hands and face. Sharon unfastened the bib-strings from behind his neck.

"And what would your argument be," she mused—arching an eyebrow because she knew it was a question I was telepathically fending off—"if someone said you were encouraging people to take dangerous risks by having babies without proper medical attention?"

"Mm." I smoothed my beard nervously. "What, indeed?"

Well, what it was at the time was a somewhat

sophistical analogy with murder mysteries and pornography. I don't think anyone seriously believes that the former stimulate readers to go out and commit murder. And the best opinion of psychiatrists seems to be that the latter has little direct influence on sexual transgressions. So, I concluded, I can jauntily dry my hands too.

Except... the more I ponder that question, the more I think it's the seat of my inquietude. I'm a liar—I *do* want people to take risks by having babies without proper medical attention. (Or at least, without what the medical Establishment would call proper attention.) I just don't want to have all the resultant mistakes and infections and deaths weighing on my frail conscience.

See? Right there is the dilemma. Life has a cutting edge, I am saying, and we should all inch out there and live on it. Come on, straddle the shimmering blade. Dangle that one leg daringly over the abyss. Okay, now try bouncing up and down a little bit... whoops!

Because when that cold steel nips into flesh, you bet I'll be the first to tumble backwards. Whimpering at the gash in my new pants and squealing for first aid.

The thing to do, I suppose, is to try to strike a balance between existential courage and foolhardiness. I mean, consider the very term "natural childbirth." It's natural for a bunch of babies to *die* from the rigors of parturition. Mothers too. If we simply let them—refusing to intervene—it would certainly be "natural"... but in an Elizabethan, archaic sense of that word, which is "idiotic." A natural, notes the OED, is one naturally deficient in intellect. But, since man is naturally gifted with an intellect, it is natural for him to use it. Thus intellectual advances in obstetrics cannot reasonably be scorned.

Then, too, what is courage and what is folly? The dilemma forks even deeper. Our decision to bring Seth into the world without assistance was based on a judicious wager. The odds, we knew, were heavily in our favor. Just ride with Nature and Nature will make her point. So there's no folly there. We were putting down a safer bet than the one we make every time we climb into the Citroen. To that extent, then—to the extent that our bet was hedged, cozy, bloodless, drained of risk—it merits no grace. Why should we think of ourselves as brave and intrepid (and here I have to admit that's the royal "we"; Sharon's attitude, I concede, has been much more organic than mine) when we undertake a venture whose success is virtually assured?

Ah, but that "virtually." For, indeed, it was a wager—and a wager always entails, no matter how minimal, the possibility of loss. Even at Cedars of Lebanon or Mt. Zion or Columbia Presbyterian or wherever the biggest and most advanced obstetrical centers are located, babies and mothers occasionally die. So there is some courage involved. And, as I believe I have made clear, it is courage of a special higher order when a woman comes to childbed like Sharon, armed only with a knowledge of what is going on in her vitals, a love for her humanity and for what it is about to produce, a willingness to experience all the dimensions of life... and maybe a few shreds of a common herb whose smoke can provide fitful comfort.

Yes, courage. But courage based on the fact that some people are going to suffer. Courage based on the fact that Nature will, from time to time, fuck up. Those stillbirths, those mental and physical deformities, those fatal hemorrhages are all essential! They've got to be there if virtue is to accrue! Without them there's no risk, and without risk no courage. That's precisely the shit-smeared pattern of life. Those of us who risk and win can never have clean hands!

See, the thing I think I failed to portray satisfactorily was just how close I really felt—just how close Sharon and Seth and I actually *were*—to tragedy. All right... to mishap, then. Death is no tragedy, but it sure can spoil your whole day. Anyway, the point is... we Americans, with our Puritan instincts, have this conviction that the wages of sin is death.

267

We bring it to bear full-bore on literature. Crime must not pay. What we fail to acknowledge, except in the conduct of our daily lives, is that the wages of sin may very well be life. And what we absolutely flail to *avoid* acknowledging—because it strikes such a fundamental terror—is the converse: Death may just as easily be the wages of the most unadulterated virtue!

It takes no great logician to abstract the moral. Life and death are not, in an ethical sense, wages. To illustrate: the parable of the broken pottery.

On the morning after Seth was born, when Sharon was sleeping and Seth was securely stuffed into an improvised crib by her side, I decided to heave a breath of fresh air. No sooner had I opened the kitchen door than I was popped cork-like through it by the sweaty, stale, emotionally carbonated brew that had been steeping behind me for the past who-knows-how-many hours. My inertia carried me across the clearing, where I wandered for a while dazzled by the brightness and the loss of enclosure and the freedom to extend my muscles and appendages haphazard. It wasn't long, though, before I noticed that the door to the pottery shed was ajar. There was a short delay until the scratch of that observation began to itch. Then I remembered its significance. I had heard something break the night before, when I angrily fired the bundle of garbage into the shed's interior darkness. I went to investigate.

I could drop in some amusing details here about how, as I approached the door, I caught a rustling from within. And about how I suddenly felt very vulnerable and panicky because of my nakedness—visions of rabid beasts darting hungrily for my genitals, nipping off cock and balls like so many juicy pears, and so on. And about how, after assuming roughly the posture made famous in "September Morn," I peered around the jamb to confront a rather demoralized raccoon. Apparently the animal had either lost track of the time—they are customarily nocturnal felons—or else had been unable to exit through the narrow opening it had entered At any rate, the raccoon accepted my invitation to flee; it zigzagged into the poison oak. I was left with the odorous task of cleaning up: four weeks' worth of organic and inorganic refuse, painstakingly rooted from its containers and conscientiously clawed and fanged into minute greasy scraps.

The crux of the story, though, lies elsewhere. In the midst of my policing I came upon the shards of fresh pottery which were what I had been seeking in the first place. If you recall, my main concern was that I might have smashed some especially ornate or unusual product of Sharon's ceramic imagination. I duck-waddled about, brushing the furthest-flung fragments back toward the epicenter. Then I squatted over my heap of geometry and tried to puzzle the original form. To give some idea of what I had to choose from, ranged above me on the open studs of the shed wall were a veritable gift-shop of air-dried items: teapots with elaborately curviform spouts and handles; tiny porcelain demitasses which would glint bone-white after firing; heavy earthenware casseroles, button-stamped and bravura-lidded; thick candleholders and abstract vases and peasant mugs and aristocratic jars and soupbowls—some of them stocky porringers, others delicate inverted bells. The colors differed too, depending on which clay-body had been used: the stonewares a leached russet, the porcelains a wan grey. The uncommon accumulation was due to the fact that Sharon has to truck all her stuff to Anita's kiln if she wants to bisque or glaze.

Anyway, faced with this variety, it took me a while to deduce that I had—to my good fortune—broken only a very run-of-the-studio soupbowl. It was, of course, what I had wanted to discover. But the evidence was supportive. The object had obviously been small, the color of the brittle shards was the same pink, and there was a gap in the soupbowl ranks just about where I calculated this victim had toppled. I swept up the remains, dropped them skittering into the trash-box and continued my garbage collection.

Well, I was telling myself, at least I won't have to mention anything to Sharon now. A soupbowl's no great loss— not like something where the shape or the concept is the most important element. A piece of art. The form here was basic. The work would derive its character, if any, from the hues and the crustings of glaze. I was supposed to feel relief. For some reason I didn't.

Physical effort often allows the mind to whirr free. And as I stooped and grunted, puffing to dredge the raccoon-spread drift out of nooks and crannies, I had a *satori*. Cruel and minor, but meaningful.

I realized I had never expected Sharon to survive.

Isn't that a terrible thing to say?

What I mean is, in my gut she was dead as soon as the first pain started. Oh yeah, in my head it was fifty-fifty... way better, of course, the odds, the more I intellectualized. But see? Ringing in the caverns of my viscera was the sound of that broken pot. All night long.... And pulsing dimly, in the furthest and most ancient galleries of my brain, was a corresponding warning light. I could and did repress it under the foreground urgencies. But still it blinked, relentless and undeniable as a distant neon sign in fog: OMEN. O.M.E.N. OMEN. OMEN.

So what did that make me?

An accessory to manslaughter. Womanslaughter... and childslaughter. Two counts. First degree.

An existential hero. Risking that which he loves most dearly—next to his own life, which tellingly was not itself in jeopardy—while refusing to be cowed by superstition.

Monster.

Exemplar.

The thing was, the terrifying, binding liberty of it all was: There's no difference.

And if Seth had been stillborn or deformed... it would only have been a soupbowl breaking. And if Sharon had died in agony... it would only have been a larger, more seasoned vase destroyed.

My fault. Not my fault. The world rattles day in and day out to the feeble crash of toppling crockery. We're so used to it we hardly ever notice.

All you can do is stumble forward in the darkness. You flings your garbage and you takes your chances.

Uh-oh. A raindrop just blew in my eye.

So much for my parable. I think I will leave all the neat parabolic finishwork to exegetes. I have an eminently curbworthy tendency to get hung up in metaphor. Meanwhile, I will gather my papers and books and prepare to dash. Satisfied that I have met the last of Sharon's objections—the last I can remember, anyway:

"Hey, Roger," she'd yelped, "did you really break one of my pieces? Without even telling me? You rat! God damn it! What was it? I can't even figure out why you've got this in here, unless it's just to get me upset...!"

"I did it because it happened," I murmured. "It's why all my stupid puns and lame jokes are still in there. All the fatuous... philosophizing... which is kind of a nice phrase, huh? Alliterates. And all my... smarmy smugness. Or whatever, however you'd characterize it. Can't say I like the way I come off when you get right down to it. Better go back and do some editing."

"Feeling a bit hard on ourselves, are we, today?"

"Not on you, I hope. You were a trouper. All the way."

"And you got me through it."

"You got yourself through it."

I can hear the rain crackling in the brush now, sharp as gunfire. But it's still sparse. The wind has faded momentarily, and the sky's thick wadding of clouds amplifies the hush. The birds and animals have disappeared to wherever birds and animals disappear when rain threatens. A while back a solitary dove was waddling around among the fallen leaves... but he's long since gone.

It occurs to me that I am going to miss such unconcerned forest companions. Not to mention the natural stillness, and the subtle violations of that stillness which I have almost come to take for granted—the electronic hum of summer sunlight, the peckish bustle of birds, the rolling echo when I slurp hot tea before the dew dries. Up here every living function vibrates clear and meaningful. And yet, in today's world that is an anomaly. Before long I will be back in the city, scuffling to earn enough bread so that we can escape again. My life too will be orchestrated by the grumble of internal combustion engines, the universal sizzle of tires on asphalt, the honking of traffic, the clatter of synthetic heels on pavement, the peculiar metallic whump as a pedestrian steps on a manhole cover. Urban, mechanical, impersonal cacophony. I just hope that's not the only world left when Seth comes of age.

Speaking of whom... I think I'll hop inside and bid a hello. It's probably getting near his nap time. He's started to gurgle lately, and I'm trying to coach him to say, *"Inter urinas et faeces nascimur."* Or, failing that, "Da-Da." I want to have him conversing intelligently by six months.

Whoa! Halfway through that last sentence I was startled by a livid electric flash and an instantaneous thunderbang. Phew, smell the ozone. I better check my eyebrows. Beard. Feel for powderburns. We don't have electrical storms around here very often, so I usually find them exciting. I get a kick out of the ruminative rumble of far-off thunder and the jagged scrawl of lightning over distant headlands. But at this range it's a little tough on the cardiovascular system. Especially when the circuit from clouds to my headpole is about twenty-five feet. And I'm distressingly negatively charged. And arranged under a tree. Perhaps it really would be smarter to get a jump on the rain.

Maybe what I'll do this afternoon is turn on. I've only smoked grass once since Seth was born. Maybe I'll throw the

I Ching for kicks. See what the future holds. Maybe I'll wade into my next project: a scholarly article for the *New England Journal of Medicine*. Probably best to do it stoned so I can get that proper hollow resonance:

"S., a healthy 23-year-old primigravida, was administered a dose of 5,000 milligrams of common Mexican cannabis sativa in the form of a cigarette during the third hour of labor...."

Here it comes!

Got to scramble to keep these pages

dry.

HEXAGRAM 17

SUI

FOLLOWING, ACCORDING WITH

...In this hexagram, the firm comes beneath the yielding; movement and joy are conjoined — hence sublime success, the reward of our persistence and freedom from error. This implies that the whole universe accords with what the times dictate for it. Great indeed is this principle of according with the pulse of time....

This hexagram symbolizes thunder rumbling within a swamp! When darkness falls, the Superior Man goes within and rests peacefully.